AND GLADLY TEACH

A Novel

By

Brian Libby

ISBN: 0-75965-404-2

This book is printed on acid-free paper.

1stBooks - rev. 8/29/01

CONTENTS

I. A LITTLE HISTORY

St. Lawrence Academy had been founded in the mid-nineteenth century by an Episcopal clergyman, Otis Cranborne, who, arriving in the Midwest when it was still quite wild, had envisioned an educational Mecca rising amidst the pine barrens of his frontier parish. At that time the town of Vacheville, founded some years before by a <u>coureur de bois</u> who had become completely lost, was home to some five hundred hearty souls, and many thought it would become the capital when the territory achieved statehood. The Rev. Mr. Cranborne had hopes of starting an elementary school, a high school, a college, and a theological seminary on the bluff overlooking the Vermillion River, not far from the cathedral already under construction.

Unfortunately Vacheville did not become the state capital, due to the eventual discovery of a somewhat larger and more navigable river than the Vermillion—namely the Mississippi—seventy-five miles away, while Mr. Cranborne's pedagogical megalomania was rudely cut short when he departed northward to convert a rather nasty Indian tribe and was never seen again. He left behind a one-room schoolhouse run by his widow.

It was the territory's first bishop, John Crozier, who saved this little school from oblivion. Seeking some way to assuage the Vachevillians (who were quite grumpy when the capital city went elsewhere and they were left with a bishopless cathedral), Bishop Crozier convinced several East Coast acquaintances to put up the cash for a boarding school whose purpose would be "to civilize and Christianize the savages." This money was used to build a massive stone building (Laud Hall) and a lovely chapel. Mrs. Cranborne's eight students became the first matriculants and St. Lawrence Academy (SLA) was born. (Despite the bishop's declared purpose, the school never enrolled any Indians. The school had been unknowingly built on a sacred burial ground and no Indian would enter it, for fear of ghosts.)

1

The chapel burned down some years later, but the bishop, one of whose ecclesiastical specialties was cozening old women, persuaded a wealthy matron in Chicago to pledge the money to rebuild it. Shortly after she made this pledge, the lady lost all her money when Chicago itself burned down; but the pious dame, faithful to her word, took her entire insurance payment and sent it to Bishop Crozier. He took it readily, leaving her to die in a poorhouse, and rebuilt the chapel, the cornerstone of which bore the quotation, "For they all have put in out of their abundance; but she out of her want has put in all that she had. (Mark 12:44)," an eternal tribute to the faith, devotion, and simplicity of Mrs. Flavia Pearsall.

The school was originally for boys, but in the 1960's, when enrollment had begun to shrink, it became coed by combining with a nearby girls' establishment, Miss Pettipaw's Lyceum. Buildings continued to rise, so that SLA's 250-acre campus eventually boasted two large dormitories, a greatly-expanded Laud Hall, the chapel, many faculty homes, assorted garages and sheds, an all-weather track, tennis courts, a golf course, and a hockey arena. The 250 students in grades nine through twelve came from thirty-seven states and nine foreign countries. The faculty came from all over. The Headmaster came from the Episcopal Church.

II. ADMISSIONS

Tuition at SLA was $21,000 per year for boarders and $14,000 for day students. Since the school was what is called "tuition-driven," (i.e its endowment wasn't big enough) it was essential to admit to capacity. Unfortunately, although SLA was very old, it was not in a part of the country with a "boarding school tradition," that is to say families in the Midwest did not readily accept the idea of paying more than what some colleges charge to send their children to a high school when they could send them to a local high school for nothing.

Mr. Leo Carter, the 33-year-old Director of Admissions, and an alumnus of SLA, was the fourth man to fill his post in seven years. (The Headmaster had little patience with people who could not admit enough students.) Mr. Carter loved SLA. He also loved getting a paycheck, and he had a wife and a young son. School was opening in a week and he was twenty-six short of the enrollment target. Mr. Carter sat with his two young admissions assistants, Linda Vail and George Potter. They were both twenty-two, hired fresh out of college to do some useful work like conducting interviews and giving tours. They were bright and eager to do well in their first real jobs. Just now they were reviewing application folders.

"How about this one?" asked George. "Morton Steinkopf. Colorado. Incoming sophomore. Likes to ski."

"Is he bringing a mountain with him?" asked Leo. "Or doesn't he know we're in the Great Plains?"

"Isn't he the one who went berserk at lunch and tried to strangle another student?" asked Linda.

"No, that was Martin Kreeger," replied George. "We've already admitted him. Morton is the one who needs two doses of Ritalin a day to keep him from running amok during classes."

There was a pause. Finally Mr. Carter asked, "What is the Steinkopfs' bottom line?"

George glanced at the last page of the folder. "Full pay," he said.

"Admit," said Leo. "Who's next?"

"Abigail Pettigill. Pasadena. Incoming junior," said George, taking up another folder. "Very good grades."

Leo looked at the transcript. "Grades in what?" he snorted. The columns indicating the courses which Miss Pettigill had taken in the ninth and tenth grades were a jumble of incomprehensible abbreviations and acronyms.

"What is LanAr?" asked Leo.

"I think it means Language Arts," said Linda.

"Is that the same as English?"

"I think so."

"And what is 'Comp Comp'?"

"Computer Competency."

"And 'Ma Con'?"

There was silence. No one knew. They did know about public schools, though. It could be something. It could be nothing. It could be anything. Another pause.

"Well, whatever it is, she got an A in it," George said hopefully.

"And a full pay," added Linda.

"Admit," said Leo. "Who's next?"

Just then there was a noise in the outer office, the door swung open all the way, and in came a man, a big man, six foot three, 220 muscular pounds, with a wild mane of dark hair, a Herculean chest, and a jaw which Mussolini would have envied: a man of tremendous power and virility, imposing, even intimidating.

"Hello, Lance," said Leo. "How's the hockey team coming along?"

III. PUCK IS A FOUR-LETTER WORD

In recent years SLA's athletic program had suffered serious setbacks. The drop in enrollment, the departure of two good coaches, and the (brief) tenure of an eccentric Headmaster who had been more interested in academics than in sports: all had caused disaster. Football, once very strong, collapsed. ("St. Lawrence roasted on gridiron," read one newspaper report.) Track, baseball, basketball, all languished. The magnificent new hockey arena, gift of hundreds of alumni, housed a weak and losing team. The athletics honor boards outside the gym, blazoned with the deathless names of the school's most illustrious sports heroes, had no entries less than a decade old.

The Board of Trustees decided that this could not go on. The Board took it for granted that athletic prowess went hand-in-hand with success in other areas and made the decision to gain dominance in at least one sport. Since the school had an ice arena, they chose hockey.

They hired a coach—the first time anyone had ever been hired solely as a coach.

Lance Vance, 41, had played professional hockey for several years. He was dynamic, magnetic, and forceful. He was handsome, charismatic, and industrious. His playing days over, he now revelled in grandiose dreams of building a hockey empire: not just one team but half a dozen; a huge summer program; an Olympic connection. Offered a three-year contract (with a salary twice what any teacher was earning) he leapt at the chance which SLA provided. His wife and kids comfortably ensconced in off-campus housing paid for by the school, Lance rolled up his sleeves and went to work.

His first task (after hiring two cronies as assistant coaches, of course) was to get a team. To facilitate this he was made an admissions officer. He admitted only hockey players. The call went out: if you can play hockey, SLA is the place for you. With

5

demonic energy (and an unlimited travel budget) Lance Vance flew to the East Coast, to the West Coast, to Toronto, to Winnipeg, to Santa Fe. Santa Fe? Indeed, yes. Even in the burning sands of America's deserts, even amidst the sagebrush and cacti of the arid Southwest, even there can hockey take root, even there can little boys be taught to skate and to shoot the puck and to hit each other with sticks. Even in Reno and Salt Lake City can the dreadful training of a hockey player begin, at the age of five or six. Even there can hand-and-eye coordination be developed at the expense of the whole rest of the brain. But to continue their training, children of the desert need a year-round facility in some snowy, more hockey-friendly clime, like Vacheville.

And so they came, a migration of Vandals and Visigoths: a subsidized migration, for they were all given financial aid, tons of it: a team recruited, bought, and paid for by Lance Vance to make SLA the premier high school hockey program in the country.

There were problems, especially in the first year. The regulations of the State High School League (SHSL), designed by and for public schools, contained all sorts of restrictions on "recruiting" and "eligibility." These regulations were not easy to understand. <u>Nothing</u> which the SHSL did was easy to understand. This organization, this "league," consisted of representatives from all the schools in the state, organized in a complicated hierarchy of districts, regions, and provinces, meeting regularly throughout the year. It considered every aspect of every sport and produced piles, heaps, Himalayas of edicts, of such turgid complexity that a team of corporate lawyers would have had trouble interpreting them. Nothing was too small or too trivial to merit the attention of the League. The weight of a basketball, the length of a baseball bat, the exact date when a football player could start practice, the yards of rubber in a golf ball: with such crucial items in the education of the young did the collective wisdom of these jock-strap Solons concern itself. But no topic received more attention than "eligibility."

6

Could a student transferring from one school to another and put back a year still play, and for how long? How about an out-of-state student? What constituted "recruiting?"

Well, if Aristotle would have had difficulty in figuring out the rulings of this athletic Areopagus, what of Lance Vance, who could barely read and write? The first year of the revivified hockey program was beset with endless difficulties with the SHSL and interminable arguments and conflicts.

The fact was, that however "recruiting" was defined, SLA was certainly doing it. But Lance Vance solved the problem. Just as Alexander the Great had overcome the difficulty of the Gordian Knot by a stroke of his sword, so Lance Vance eliminated the interference of the SHSL by removing SLA Hockey from the League. By such boldness are great men known. In exchange for a few trifling annoyances, such as ineligibility to play in any state tournaments, SLA's stickmen were free to recruit like mad and play all the games they wanted, all over the country, even with Junior League and college freshmen teams. Lance planned one hell of a season: fifty, sixty, maybe seventy games, travel almost every weekend, play until the end of April. The prospects were exciting: national recognition, fame, more recruits for the summer camp, whee!

The first season had been a great success. Lance Vance's tough little mercenaries had gone through the opposition like the Wehrmacht had gone through Poland. The coming years would be even greater. Hockey über Alles!

But Lance Vance's appearance in the admissions office occasioned no euphoria among the three people already there. They knew what was coming.

"Got three new players, I mean students," boomed Lance. "Best goalie in Arizona, a great center from Ottawa, and wait'll you see this guy from Anchorage. Would you believe a ninth-grader six feet one and 210 pounds?"

"How many years has he been in the ninth grade?" asked George, who liked Lance even less than did most people.

"Just one," replied Lance, handing him a folder from his expensive attaché case. "I think he'll be coming in on the 'Lawrence Plan,' though."

"So he'll repeat the ninth grade here," muttered Leo, glancing at the transcript. "Which makes sense, seeing that he flunked everything in Alaska."

"Not math," said Lance. "He got a C in that."

"The teacher must have been easy to cheat off of," whispered George to Linda.

"Well, just stopped in to give you guys the good news," said Lance. "I'm off to Las Vegas this afternoon." He left.

Leo, Linda, and George looked at each other silently. Almost all the people Lance admitted were induced to come to SLA through financial aid. It was necessary to admit more full-pays to compensate for the fact that the hockey players paid an average of only two-thirds tuition.

Linda picked up another folder. "Holly Zeigler. Incoming sophomore. Low test scores. D+ average. Dressed like a hooker when she came for her interview. Parents going through a divorce and can't handle her at home."

"Full pay?"

"Yes."

"Admit."

IV. ENCOURAGING WORDS

The school year always began with a series of faculty meetings, at the first of which the Headmaster would deliver a speech to set the tone for the year ahead and to apprise his subordinates of what items were currently uppermost in his mind.

"We must always keep in mind that our children are students, not alduts."

The Headmaster was 47, with metallic gray hair, a resonant voice, and eyes similar to those of Rasputin.

"Remember, also, that, although we are not here to correct major behaviors, we are in loco parientibus for these young people. They often need motivation. Many come to us from dysfanctional fumilies, or, given the high national divorce rate, from single-family households. A boarding school is a twenty-four-hour operation."

Some of the teachers in the back row were exchanging glances, and two or three were biting their tongues. But none would have thought of interrupting the Headmaster, let alone of laughing. To do so would have been as unthinkable as for a peasant to have interrupted Louis XIV.

"We must strive to minister to our students' needs at all times. We must sometimes kick them in the butt and love them to death simultaneously. Remember, the 'squeaky wheel' may get more out of the school experience than the good student."

The Headmaster had reached his peroration, his disturbing eyes wide behind his glasses. "Above all, never forget that parents have entrusted to us their most precious possession: their money, I mean their children. In short, we must ceaselessly strive to become the kind of school which, to some extent, we already are."

The Headmaster sat down. The Director of Studies, staring at the table he was sitting behind, said, "We'll take a ten-minute break. Please be back on time."

The thirty-seven teachers in the crowded room got up and stretched. Mr. Vetter, one of the four math teachers, glanced at the Headmaster, turned to his science colleague Mr. del Rey, and whispered, "Do you have any idea what in hell he's talking about?"

Mr. del Rey, who had been at SLA for twenty-nine years and had seen several Headmasters come and go, smiled and said, "Of course not. But don't worry, Bill—neither does he."

V. THE MAGI

As part of the opening week's meetings, the faculty was introduced to Dr. Rodney L. Glennis, the founder and president of the firm of Broad Horizons, Inc., educational consultants. SLA had hired Broad Horizons to study all aspects of school life and to recommend ways to attract more students, reduce expenses, and, in general, make more money. (As a non-profit organization SLA was naturally very concerned with making as much money as possible.)

What is a "consultant"? The dictionary says, "an expert who is called on for professional or technical advice," but a far more comprehensive definition might be "someone who is paid a lot of money to figure out things you ought to be able to figure out for yourself." Another definition, apt for the sort of consultant the educational world produces, is "someone who, not liking to be a teacher or an an administrator, now makes more money than either by telling them how to teach and administrate."

The world of education teems with consultants, it seethes with them, it is lousy with them. There is probably no school in the country whose substance has not been drained by at least one of these academic lampreys. It is not easy to say why communities consisting of well-educated adults, with decades of experience in every aspect of their profession, shell out thousands of dollars to these self-proclaimed experts. But they do. In the private school world there are even consultants to whom parents can go for the purpose of finding the "right" school for their child. This is a particularly lucrative field, since parents driven to use such services are so desperate to get their kid(s) out of the house that they will pay any amount to find a school which will take them. Such consultants, with just a computer, a phone, a copy of the Bunting & Lyon guide, and a knowledge of which schools are in financial trouble, could place Jack the Ripper in a private school, for a suitable fee.

11

Dr. Glennis (exactly what he was a doctor of was not clear, but the title engendered confidence in his clients) was a tall, gaunt, balding man in his late fifties, with bushy brows and bright brown eyes. He had arrived with a staff of three and several suitcases full of charts, tables, graphs, and overheads. He spoke for two solid hours. He painted an unnerving picture of the future. He explained how American teenagers were with each passing minute becoming stupider, lazier, and more undisciplined, how their parents were becoming less and less competent at raising them, how independent schools would soon be inundated with these creatures, and how any school which hoped to survive would have to develop "new and innovative programs," "a clearer vision of viable objectives," and "a distinctive cachet to proclaim itself unique among the profusion of similar institutions."

All the while he spoke, his aides were busy flashing transparencies on the screen and whisking them away before the squinting audience could deduce their meaning, if indeed they had any. One chart was displayed upside-down, but that really made no difference.

"Broad Horizons has been conducting an in-depth study of SLA, which will be concluded shortly. We will then be in a position to make further recommendations as to how you can improve recruitment and retention. You have already taken a great step forward by energizing your hockey program, as I recommended to the Board two years ago."

"So it's his fault," whispered several of the teachers.

"SLA cannot rest on its academics. Remember, parents take for granted that every independent school has an excellent teaching staff, superb courses, unlimited individual attention, and fine college preparatory opportunities. That's a given."

Now many teachers were glancing at each other. Was this true? Were parents really that dumb?

"What you must have is a further extra-curricular, I mean co-curricular, ..." Dr. Glennis's volubility momentarily stopped. The word he had almost used, "gimmick," didn't seem elevated

12

enough. Then he went on, "... dimension. which will individualize your identity. You must not be thought of as a 'plain vanilla' school, but rather as a Neapolitan one, a sort of tutti-frutti, which offers things unique, distinctive, <u>sui generis</u>!"

The teachers didn't clap, partly because they were mostly appalled, and partly because they did not know he was done. But he was done, for the moment.

In the back row Mr. Vetter turned to Mr. del Rey. "But I <u>like</u> vanilla," he whispered plaintively.

Mr. Jones, the European History teacher, a crabbed and reactionary man who had a particularly low tolerance for consultants, and indeed for innovations in general, looked at his schedule and noted with regret that tomorrow another speaker would appear. Mr. Jones often wondered who did this scheduling. He thought it was done by the Senior Staff, or SS, at its weekly meeting. The term SS did not mean—as one might think—those members of the faculty who had been at SLA for the longest time. No, the SS was an ex officio group which did not include any full-time teachers. Exactly who it did include was hard to say. Mr. Jones had never seen any list which specified the members of the Senior Staff. The SS exercised power anonymously, like the Venetian Council of Ten, the Neapolitan Camarilla, and the Illuminati. Perhaps the members had a secret handshake or a special tie clip. At any rate, these ghostly councillors seemed to be responsible for bringing to the campus the succession of quacks, mountebanks, and assorted humbugs who periodically bedevilled the busy teachers with their crackpot theories and impractical advice.

On the morrow, the latest speaker turned out to be some sort of child psychologist, an adolescent development "expert." His presentation was so bizarre that many of the teachers wondered if it was an elaborate practical joke, similar to the one at a convention some years before where the keynote speaker, billed as Margaret Thatcher's educational advisor and the youngest pilot to have flown with the RAF in the Battle of Britain, turned out to be a comedian. Certainly the clouds of jargon which befogged the room had about them an aura of comic implausibility.

First came something called the "Optimal Environmental Conditions" (which made Mr. Jones think of seventy degrees and low humidity,) which were engendered by a teacher having "Congruent Anticipatory Sets" with his students. This led, somehow, to "Cognitive Behavioral Change." Intervention in student discipline would succeed, said the speaker, only if "environmental conditions" were "appropriate." One had to "assess the lethality" of a situation so that one could provide "value-added opportunities" which students would "buy into."

With everyone reeling from this barrage, the speaker—Dr. somebody, they were always "doctors"—physician, heal thyself—went on to the topic of "Gaining a Meta-Perspective." A "teacher-student interaction" was something which happened on the "subjective level." When the teacher then discussed this "interaction" with one or more colleagues, he gained a "meta-perspective." A discussion of this discussion furnished one with a "meta-meta-perspective." And ...

Mr. Jones quietly got up and went away. He knew that he might be reprimanded for this desertion, but he thought that a reprimand would be preferable to being jailed for murdering the speaker, which, given his state of mind, was his only alternative to departure. On his way home he marvelled, not for the first time, at his colleagues' patience in tolerating these verbal assaults. He knew that SLA was not unique. All over the country, probably all over the world, these "experts" were going to and fro in the earth, and walking up and down in it, chanting their incomprehensible mantras to captive audiences at conventions, school openings, and faculty meetings, and being well-paid for doing so.

At least, thought Mr. Jones as he entered his apartment and sank into his easy chair, this guy hadn't had us "break up into little groups." That was a favorite technique of those people. The faculty would be divided into squads of five or six and sent hither and yon to discuss some problem concocted by the speaker. Often each group would be instructed to write its collective thoughts with a magic marker on large, poster-sized sheets of paper. When the faculty reconvened, the speaker would pin up the sheets of paper all around the room, so it resembled a kindergarten, and then everyone would compare the various ideas and try to find "congruence." After it was found—and it always was—the now-congruent teachers could go home, the speaker would gather up the posters and throw them away, and no one would ever hear or speak of the matter again. This was called a "very productive meeting."

Looking at the school calendar, Mr. Jones saw that in two weeks the faculty would hear from a firm of architects. He smiled wryly. This would be the third or fourth architectural presentation in about as many years. The Headmaster and the Board were always coming up with wonderful plans for renovating the dorms and classrooms, erecting new buildings, and generally modernizing the campus. This led (of course) to hiring a consultant, who, in return for a few tens of thousands of dollars, would produce plans of striking beauty and marvellous utility. These beautiful plans would be displayed at a faculty meeting and explained by a voluble expert who would make it seem as if paradise would come as soon as the school built the magnificent structures so carefully delineated on his expensive charts.

Mr. Jones recalled the plan for the huge field house connected to Laud Hall by an aerial walkway; the completely-renovated boys' dorm, with its suites and lounges; the new main entrance to the school, which would have made coming to SLA an experience similar to that of arriving at Versailles. Ah, yes, they were all so wonderful...

The only problem was that none of them was ever built. SLA had barely enough money to perform the routine maintenance required to keep its existing buildings from falling to the ground. Starting work on the architects' plans depended on a successful Capital Campaign, and this campaign, for which (of course) consultants had been repeatedly hired and paid more tens of thousands of dollars, never started. It never started because the consultants said that one does not <u>start</u> a capital campaign until <u>after</u> half the money has already been raised quietly and behind the scenes, so as to convince prospective donors that the whole amount would indeed be collected, and so far the SLA Board and alumni who were solicited had not promised enough.

And so the architectural plans remained, insubstantial and fairylike: pleasure-domes decreed but never built, until replaced by other, newer, ephemeral drawings and evanescent figments of imagination.

Mr. Jones reflected that if the Headmaster and the Board could remove the opium pipes from their teeth and come down to planet Earth, they might take all the money spent on these consultants and just do something useful with it, like repairing the scandalously decrepit boys' showers. In thinking this, however, Mr. Jones was merely demonstrating that he would never be a Headmaster, because he lacked "Strategic Vision." Strategic Vision is the ability to ignore mundane realities completely and to immerse oneself in a world of dreams. All great educational leaders have it.

As for Mr. Jones, well, he really felt, after being exposed to all these consultants, advisors, and experts, that a school in need of guidance would be better off if it hired an astrologer. The fees would be less, and the advice every bit as reliable.

VI. AD MAJOREM DEI GLORIAM

The chapel at SLA was a lovely stone building with stained-glass windows and an imposing spire. Visitors entering it for the first time were always surprised to see that the pews faced each other across a single central aisle. (This was a feature modeled on school chapels in England, the spiritual home of every real American boarding school.) This unusual layout meant that the two halves of the congregation faced each other rather than the altar, and a modicum of thought might have led the architects to realize that such an arrangement was probably not the best one for an audience consisting largely of teenagers. Still, it was a nice oddity for campus tour guides to talk about.

The turnover in school chaplains was high. The average one lasted about three years. This was due in part to the nature of the ministry. The freedom of religion enjoyed by citizens of civilized countries has, as one of its many beneficial effects, the result that church congregations consist largely of people who want to be there, and consequently a modern pastor can usually depend upon the cooperation and receptivity of his flock.

At religious boarding schools, however, things are otherwise. If services were voluntary, they could be held in a phone booth. The students at SLA were not selected on the basis of their being Episcopalians, or Christians, or believers at all. But all students were required to attend Sunday chapel. Catholics, Jews, Buddhists, agnostics, atheists: all were herded together and given God's word straight out of the <u>Book of Common Prayer</u>.

Such a congregation was not a pastor's dream. Any sort of active participation was very hard to get from these involuntary worshippers, and the amount of inattention, whispering, gum-chewing, etc. was hard to bear. Many chaplains were finally worn out by the indifference.

Ignorance was also a debilitating influence. Most of the students were Christians of some sort. It said so on their application forms. It did not seem, however, that their Christianity included any sort of religious education subsequent to their baptism. It was really amazing. Students came to SLA without the slightest knowledge of the most basic beliefs held by the faiths to which they purportedly belonged. Many would have had difficulty in differentiating between Jesus and Jupiter. Each year, when Mr. Jones began his Modern Europe course with the Reformation, he discovered "Catholics" who had no idea what Purgatory was, "Presbyterians" who had never heard of Calvin, "Lutherans" who did not know what country Martin Luther came from, and "Episcopalians" who were surprised to learn that their sect was somehow connected to the "Anglican" faith. It was not unknown for a student, on the matching section of the first Modern Europe quiz, to put "Ignatius Loyola" as the answer to "He founded Lutheranism."

The St. Lawrence faculty was not selected on the basis of religious belief, either, and, being a group of well-educated modern adults, about half of them were atheists, agnostics, or deists of some sort. They were required to go to chapel, too, if they were on duty on a given Sunday. (Someone had to maintain order and take attendance so absentees could be punished.)

The previous year had been the last one for the incumbent chaplain, an older man known to the students as "Father Sominex." His demise had occurred after the Director of Studies, passing by the cleric's classroom one afternoon, beheld the entire class dozing while the priest, unaware or unconcerned that his audience was unconscious, droned on about the Book of Numbers. (His departure had not hurt his career. On the contrary: his accomplished pulling of strings inside the Episcopal hierarchy had gained him the Headmastership of a school in Connecticut.) In hiring his replacement, SLA had sought a younger, dynamic, vigorous man. They had found one in the Rev. Asmodeus Clovenhoof.

18

Although only recently ordained, Fr. Clovenhoof was in his mid-thirties, for his vocation had come to him a trifle late in life, as is so often the case with the Episcopalian clergy. Having tried, without much success, real estate, retail sales, and managing a Dairy Queen, he had suddenly been inspired, doubtless by the Holy Ghost, to devote his life to God (or at least to become a priest.)

This apparently sudden shift to God from Mammon was not, in fact, as radical as it might seem. Asmodeus Clovenhoof had always been fascinated by things spiritual, mystical, and otherworldly. This had begun when his parents had given him a ouija board when he was six, and it progressed through the I Ching and the Tarot to astrology and, finally, magic. Indeed, one reason he had failed at commerce—for he lacked neither brains nor ambition—was his unwillingness to spare much time for mere mundane pursuits. He had assembled an impressive collection of rare tomes and grimoires, which he studied assiduously, and he began to hanker for the prestige and respect of a guru, shaman, or something similar. It had not occurred to him, though, that any extant religion could accommodate his eclectic theology.

Then he looked at the Protestant Episcopal Church of the U.S.A. What a revelation! What a surprise! He discovered that, right before his eyes, there was a faith which could accommodate the most varied beliefs. Asmodeus Clovenhoof could hardly credit his good luck in finding an old, respectable, quite literally "established" church which had room for proponents of every heresy known since Arian. The famous mage Aleister Crowley could have written a motto for this church: "Do what thou wilt shall be the whole of the law."

Into this "heaven-sent" refuge scurried Asmodeus Clovenhoof, a star pupil at his seminary (where his thesis, Yahweh and Satan, Two Aspects of God, had won warm approval for its daring speculations.) He had had little difficulty in finding a bishop willing to ordain so audacious a theologian as himself. Father Clovenhoof lived in a cottage near the chapel and was settling in well. His bookshelves were full, the writings of Augustus and Aquinas next to the <u>Grand Grimoire of Honorius</u> and the <u>Scripta Majora</u> of Hermes Trismegistus, and he was busy preparing his sermon for the opening chapel service.

VII. DEVELOPMENT

While most of the school community was busy getting ready for school to open, the Development Director and his staff were busy trying to make sure it did not close. Located in the basement of Laud Hall, the Development Department comprised the Director, two Associate Directors, and three secretaries. There were over 5,000 living SLA alumni, and keeping track of them all was a lot of work.

To be an "alumnus/a" of SLA was much easier than to be a "graduate." Student turnover was quite high, with students throughout the year leaving voluntarily, flunking out, or being expelled. But even if a new student spent just one term at the school, he was an official alumnus, eligible for the rest of his life to receive fund-raising letters, phonathon calls, and, should he become rich, the personal attention of the Development Director.

The incumbent of this vital office was Mario Pestalozzi, who had been at the school only for a year. Mr. Pestalozzi, 47, had come from a background in public relations with an olive oil company in Chicago, where he had doubled the firm's clients in just three years. The arrival of his resumé at SLA had caused no little surprise, for it seemed unusual that so successful a businessman from a large city would want a position at a small school in the country. But when he had come for his interview Mr. Pestalozzi had explained that he was tired of Chicago's weather—"It's getting too hot for me there," he had said—and wanted to raise his family of six in a safe, clean, rural environment. His application was accepted with gratitude.

Traditional development work requires immense patience, tact, craft, and guile. A good D.D. must have the affability of a Welcome Wagon hostess and the diplomatic skills of a Metternich. The tuition at SLA, large though it was, covered only about eighty per cent of expenses. The rest had to come from other sources, primarily the alumni. The annual phonathon netted about one-fourth of the necessary cash. The rest (and, of course, far more, if possible) had to be wangled out of rich people.

Quite a number of alumni were rich. Many came from wealthy families and had inherited fortunes. Others were successful in business, medicine, or law. One was a famous actress. The money was there, all right. The challenge was to get these plutocrats to give some to the school. Not every alum liked SLA. Many were crotchety and hard to deal with. Some of the men were still upset that the school had dropped its Junior ROTC program and failed to understand that a military component was not a helpful thing to have in the Vietnam era. Many women still recalled with nostalgia the days when Miss Pettipaw's Lyceum had been a separate institution and unfavorably contrasted their fond memories of a cultured finishing school for young ladies of good breeding with the uncouth hoydens they now saw at the school on their alumni weekends.

Even more frustrating than these reluctant givers were the people who promised substantial sums in their wills and then did not die. There were many millions of dollars awaiting SLA, in trust funds, restricted gifts, and bequests, pending the demise of various elderly people all over the country. But pledging posthumous money to SLA seemed to act like a wonder drug. Superannuated graybeards who told the school they were leaving it half a million continued to spin out their days in peace and health. Feeble crones whose safety deposit boxes contained stacks of treasury bills destined for SLA suddenly felt rejuvenated and signed up for tap-dancing lessons. One palsied nonagenarian who had shown the D.D. a trust for two million dollars was featured in the national news several years later receiving congratulations from the President on his centenary.

It was downright maddening, and not only because time moved too slowly. One could never tell what catastrophes lurked in wait. The best-laid plans, etc. Only three years back a frail patriarch who enjoyed boasting that when he died SLA would be covered in gold was ensnared by his young housekeeper, who married him and got every drop of the eagerly-awaited Danaean shower. Disasters like this shortened the lives of Development Directors.

Mario Pestalozzi did not intend to become prematurely gray because of such contretemps. Leaving his two young assistants, who were both alumni, to handle the Phonathon and the routine giving, he set out on the quest of what he called "the big bucks." Mr. Pestalozzi was a large, heavily-built man who shaved twice a day. He exuded an aura of intimidating menace which had been of great help to him in his Chicago career and which was proving equally beneficial in his work for SLA. His visits to alumni were usually very successful. After the showing of the current school film, some discussion of the importance of education, and often a rambling reminiscence by the alum about the good old days, Mario would smile broadly, the light glinting off his gold-capped front teeth, lay a ham-sized hand on the prospective donor's shoulder, and say, "Now, Mr. X., how much can your alma mater count on from you?" This resolute approach normally worked, even with strong-willed business executives much older than he. Many a prospect, indeed, felt suddenly and unprecedentedly generous, as though the size of his contribution might well determine if he came out of the interview in one piece. Mario Pestalozzi was bringing back thousands of dollars. But he was still not really content. He wanted millions, and the really big bucks were tied up in the vaults of cranky misers and in posthumous bequests.

One afternoon in September Mario was in conference with Mary Coster and John Fordiss, his assistants, when a secretary brought in a phone message. Mario groaned after reading it.

"What's wrong?" asked young Mary.

"This is from Jake Winters, our alumni rep in California," said Mario, his hand on his forehead. "You know Arthur Hobart, the retired light bulb magnate?"

"The one who's leaving us $1.4 million?"

23

"Not any more. My God ... Jake says that Hobart is getting interested in weird religions and he's now planning to leave his whole fortune to the Rosicrucians."

Both Mary and John gasped as the scope of this disaster sank in. After a while John said, "Gee, I wish there was some kind of consultant we could use."

Mario, now holding his head in both hands, looked at his eager young aide through his fingers. "A consultant?" he echoed.

"Yes—some expert who could help us find a way to get the money we've been promised."

Mario sat up. "John, you're a genius. Why didn't I think of that?"

"You know of someone?" asked Mary.

"Oh, si, I mean yeah, I sure do. I got some, uh, business associates in Chitown who could help us a whole lot. Funny, I never thought of using 'em in this line of work. Oh, yeah, I can see it all now ..." He rose. "From now on there's no <u>scemo innato</u>, no <u>stupido vecchio rincitrullito</u>, who's gonna finagle us out of our cash. John, book me a flight to Chicago for tomorrow. I'm going to get us some <u>real good</u> consultants!"

VIII. OPENING WEEK

The students had arrived and school had begun. Each year about half of SLA's students were new, a percentage really far too high for the sort of stability and continuity which an old boarding school demands. The usual pattern was for parents to allow their child to finish grade nine in junior high and then, not wishing to send him to the local high school, enroll him in SLA. But other parents took a year or more to figure out how bad their public school was, so a good many students arrived in grade eleven. The freshman class, which should of course have been the biggest, was the smallest.

A lot of students arrived during the year, even as late as January. Schools having financial problems cannot stop admitting, and so at SLA, as in the Temple of Janus, the doors were open most of the time. This was not a desirable situation, of course. Aside from the lack of continuity resulting from many new students arriving several weeks into the courses, midyear admissions were fraught with difficulties. Mr. Carter and his staff needed superhuman prescience to decide which October and November applicants should be admitted.

The problem was that when a prospective student suddenly applied in midterm, the odds were about five to one that he shouldn't be admitted, but the parents were usually so anxious to get rid of the kid that they were even more mendacious than parents usually were about their progeny. They would do anything to gain admission. Dreadful hoods thrown out of public schools—and anyone who contrives to be thrown out of a public school is someone who would make Al Capone look like Little Lord Fauntleroy—would be passed off as persecuted, misunderstood foundlings who just needed a fresh start. Budding drug tsars would be described as innocent waifs. Dyslexics who couldn't spell their own names would have all documentary evidence of their malady—which SLA was in no

25

way prepared to handle—suppressed by their guileful parents. It took the wisdom of Solomon to decide if some pleasant, well-dressed young lady arriving for an interview was in fact a decent student who had just decided a bit late to bail out of an inferior public school, or if it was a case of her folks not wanting to be around when their daughter made her next suicide attempt. But SLA needed the money, so midyear admissions were a fact of life.

For the students on hand for the opening days there was a rapid orientation followed by the start of classes. Every year the administration discussed at length how many days should be devoted to introducing new students to the school, but no good number was ever found. The fact is that living at a boarding school is so unnatural for American teenagers that it took weeks and weeks for most to adjust. Whether they had one or two or three "orientation" days made little difference, so it was thought best just to assign them a dorm room, send them to class, and give 'em hell.

One orientation activity had remained for quite a while: the Ropes Course. A former Dean of Students, who had been to one too many leadership conferences, was inspired to build, with the use of student labor provided by those in detention, a sort of obstacle course behind the golf links. It was divided into fourteen stations, including balancing exercises, Tarzan-like swinging problems, "trust fall" platforms, and a fourteen-foot-high wooden wall. The students would be divided into teams of ten or twelve, each led by one or two faculty members, and sent out to negotiate each station. This was supposed to build school spirit and cooperation among students of different ages.

Casualties were usually acceptable: a few sprained ankles, a bit of rope burn, a concussion or two, an occasional case of heat exhaustion. Little ninth-grade girls, terrified out of their wits, being boosted (or if necessary thrown) over the wall by brawny seniors; middle-aged teachers trying to avoid being crippled before classes began: all this was, of course, good, clean fun, and it did make the whole rest of the year seem easier. Alas, the

Ropes Course was short-lived, for one day the school's liability insurance agent toured the campus, took a look at the Wall and the Trust Fall platforms, and fainted. After that the Ropes Course was used only by the summer hockey camps.

Classes at SLA were forty-five minutes long, with four in the morning and three in the afternoon, five days a week. The class day began at 8:00 and ended at 2:45, followed by thirty-five minutes of extra help, except on Monday, when a fifteen-minute assembly pushed the ending to 3:35, on Tuesday, when a twenty-minute small convocation pushed it to 3:40, and on Thursday, when all classes were shortened to forty minutes to allow for a forty-five minute large convocation. The daily periods were numbered 1 through 7, and they met in that order on Monday. On Tuesday the order was 2, 3, 4, 5, 6, 7, 1; on Wednesday, 3, 4, 5, 6, 7, 1, 2; on Thursday, 4, 5, 6, 7, 1, 2, 3; and on Friday, 5, 6, 7, 1, 2, 3, 4. Every third Wednesday classes began at 10:00 and were shortened to thirty minutes so the faculty could get to school at 8:00 and spend two hours in meetings of various kinds. On holy days, which the Chaplain could declare whenever he liked (such as the Feast of Catherine of Siena,) classes were forty minutes and a fifty-minute chapel period was inserted between the second and third hours.

This logical schedule encouraged regularity and order.

IX. IF YOU CAN READ THIS, THANK A TEACHER

The faculty members at SLA were about as normal a bunch of adults as one could find anywhere and smarter than most groups. There were thirty-seven of them; they ranged in age from twenty-three to sixty; twenty-two were men; most had M.A.'s from good schools; most were married. There were a lot of faculty children, fifteen being under age six. The whole faculty lived on campus: twelve were dormitory houseparents while the rest resided in various detached houses, cottages, and hovels. It was to quite an extent a closed community. SLA was not very popular in the town, and the school was in many ways a world of its own: one of those microcosms you hear about.

Of course a considerable number of local people worked at SLA.   The clerical staff and the kitchen employees, the groundsmen, carpenters, painters, and engineers, all came from Vacheville and surrounding villages, and many had been there as long, and were as devoted to the school, as the older faculty members.

In the early 1980's one of the consultants hired for that year had the job of trying to teach the Board of Trustees about education.   This was thought desirable because none of the Board members had anything to do with the teaching profession. The consultant's report had contained the following:

> Dr. Gerber attempted to describe for the Board the nature of an independent school. He first described the faculty as a strange breed. They work for virtually no money, they like kids, and they have hours and duties extended far beyond those of any other workers. There is an intensity to the job which is required for few other positions... . There is a lack of individual life, a lack of

28

social life. and this contributes to the high burn-out factor among boarding school teachers. He asked why anyone in his right mind would work for low compensation on a 24-hour basis while creating no equity for himself.

That summed things up rather neatly. These teachers, all of whom had plenty of brains, were toiling at jobs which made virtually any other work done by educated people seem easy. When school was in session there was no letup. Saturdays and Sundays, national holidays, went by almost unnoticed. Teachers coached sports, they chaperoned trips, they spent hours supervising study halls and detention. They ran dormitories, putting their students to bed at 10:45 on school nights and midnight on weekends. They ate their meals with students, ran clubs and activities, gave extra help every day, often including Sunday nights. They advised students, cared for them, brought them up.

Oh, yes: the teachers also taught classes, four or five per day—sometimes six. Teaching one class well can require the forensic skill, quick thinking, adaptability, and stamina that a lawyer would use in an important case; but a lawyer argues only a few such cases a year, not twenty-five times a week, and a lawyer has a more receptive audience.

SLA faculty had no "tenure." That word is never used in independent schools. Everyone at SLA worked on one-year contracts, and these contracts contained a clause stating "this agreement may be cancelled at any time by either party by a thirty-day notice." Any teacher who had been at SLA for twenty years had signed twenty such contracts, year by year. If a teacher left SLA, he lost his house, of course. The few people who stayed at the school long enough to retire often spent their "golden years" in trailers or one-room apartments.

And yet somehow, for some reason, these men and women, day after day, week after week, tried their best to make civilized and educated adults out of the coarse and ignorant children entrusted to their care. And, surprisingly, they often succeeded.

X. OPENING CHAPEL

The first chapel service of the year was always an eye-opening experience for new students, most of whom had never seen Anglo-Catholicism in all its glory. Services—some chaplains actually called them Masses—were conducted with a High Church grandeur which would have warmed the heart of King Charles I. The chaplain was assisted by the Student Vestry, and these students naturally wanted to stage as big a production as possible.

A rather long organ prelude began each service while the Vestry formed up in the vestibule. Then the organist was signalled, by an electric bell, to switch to the opening hymn. The Hymnal had a lot of good tunes in it, and there is nothing like "Rise, Up, O Men of God" or "Stand Up, Stand Up for Jesus" to get a congregation on its feet. As the singing began, there came down the aisle—which, you will recall, was faced by the parallel pews—the crucifer, in red and white, carrying a huge gilded crucifix atop a wooden pole (a piece of faux baroque craftsmanship which would not have looked out of place in a Papal procession), two surpliced acolytes with lighted candles in ornate holders, and six gowned students, each carrying a large flag on its pole: the Stars and Stripes and the state flag, the Episcopal flag and the diocesan flag, the SLA flag and the Lyceum flag. (Episcopalians just _love_ flags.) After all these came the Verger, in a black cassock and cardinal-red sash, carrying his badge of office, a sort of marshal's baton tipped with a cross. Then came the whole school choir, the Senior Warden with the book of the Gospels, and last the officiant in full pontificals.

Once this imposing cortege had entered the sanctuary through the altar rail and disposed itself on the appropriate benches, the service began. This always followed the Book of Common Prayer verbatim. This imitation Catholic Mass, in its imitation Catholic church, was periodically interspersed with hymns which, for some reason, had to be sung in extenso, sometimes six or seven verses, interminable things (for there is no type of music which seems longer than a hymn.) Many of these were of unusual provenance. Mr. Jones, the European History teacher, was delighted to discover himself singing the German national anthem (with different words, of course) when Hymn 385 came up, and he wondered if Haydn, who wrote the music (also to different words) would have liked "Sion, city of our God" better than "unser guter Kaiser Franz," or if Hoffman von Fallersleben, whose words are the most famous (or infamous) to be set to Papa Haydn's music, would have thought "Safe they feed upon the manna which he gives them when they pray" less stirring than "Deutschland, Deutschland über alles, über alles in der Welt." The children's hymn "I Sing a Song of the Saints of God" was sometimes used, the words "You can meet them in trains, or in shops, or at tea" sounding a bit out of place in American mouths. Then there was "All Things Bright and Beautiful," which called on the faithful to rejoice that God had made "each little flower that opens, each little bird that sings," while ignoring the less pleasant entities for which He Who Made All was presumably also responsible.

The Headmaster, who always attended chapel (and occasionally officiated), and sat in a special ornate chair at the front, was for some reason, probably an inconvenient phone call, late to this opening service. It began anyway with all four rousing verses of that great hymn entitled "423." "Immortal, invisible, God only wise," sang the students and teachers. (Mr. Jones wondered what "God only wise" meant, but reflected that one of the nice things about hymns was that nobody cared what they said, even if it was gibberish or, as in this case, the phrasing of another era now obscure in this one. All that mattered was the tune.) The Headmaster happened to enter just as the congregation was belting out the last verse, and walked to his throne to the words

32

Thou reignest in glory, thou rulest in light; Thine angels adore Thee, all veiling their sight;

All laud we would render, O help us to see; 'tis only the splendor of light hideth Thee.

It was clear from the opening gun (or bell) that this year chapel would be different from what it had been before (i.e., boring.) Father Clovenhoof was a small man, five and a half feet tall, with thick black hair, a triangular face, and a tiny spade beard. Wearing a white amice and a flame-red cope (which was uncanonical, but he couldn't resist) he made an unforgettable picture coming down the aisle, and in the next hour he took advantage of those parts of the service which allowed any creativity to impress his personality on his new flock. His homily, delivered in his soft but clear voice while he paced up and down the central aisle, asserted that Jesus Christ had never explicitly claimed to be the son of God—even his answers to Pilate's questions were equivocal. At the dismissal, he told the people to bow their heads and close their eyes. He then pushed a button on the small tape recorder he had placed inside the pulpit and dulcet bells began to sound softly through the church. "Take your problems," came Fr. Clovenhoof's soothing voice, "your troubles and temptations .... imagine you are standing on a dock with all your difficulties piled up beside you....take them and put them into a sack, a big burlap bag....now you are putting that sack into the boat at the dock....you cast loose its hawser...." Ding, ding, ding went the taped Buddhist temple bells. "It's drifting downstream, it's drifting away....the little boat with all your worries on board....you watch it go....go forever....it's gone....may the Lord bless you and keep you, may He make His face to shine upon you and be gracious to you. In the name of Yaweh, who is Jehova, who is I Am That Am, Ipsissimus, Belphegor and the Lord of All Desires, amen, amen, amen, fiat, fiat, fiat." Ding, dong, ding ding.

33

Then suddenly came the grand recessional, to the tune of "Onward, Christian Soldiers," and a lot of dazed and mildly befuddled people went out into the afternoon sun.

XI. CLASS

At five classes a day for 160 class days a teacher is on stage 800 times per year, for about 600 hours. This time is backed by many hours of planning and preparation and endless grading. All this, at a boarding school, is only a portion of the total workload. Many teachers considered a day on which they only had to teach five classes, do some grading, and prep the next day's classes to be an easy day, a trifle almost. If, after the class day, and giving extra help, one did not have to spend two hours coaching a sport, and then, after supper, do dorm duty until 11 PM, one had it made.

Yet despite all the calls on their time, all the faculty considered teaching the most important thing. Most of what was of lasting value at SLA took place between 8 AM and 3 PM in the rather decrepit classrooms of Laud Hall. (True, some alumni asserted that the most important parts of their time at SLA were the friendships they had made or the sports they had played, but such people were usually pretty dumb.)

It is 8:50 AM on a Tuesday in the winter term, the start of Period 3. Mr. Jones waits for the bell to ring. The nineteen students in this Modern Europe section are on time and more or less in proper dress. (SLA has a dress code, not a uniform. Mr. Jones, whose mind is on the class he's about to teach, would notice only a major dress violation, like jeans or sneakers.)

The bell rings. "OK, let's get started." Everyone is quiet. Mr. Jones goes to the bookcase and takes a handful of slips of paper off the top. "We'll start with a reading quiz." Groans arise. One boy says smugly, "I knew it." The slips are distributed.

"There are three questions. First, what, collectively, were the Cisalpine, Ligurian, Batavian, Parthenopean, and Helvetic Republics?"

35

Since this barrage of odd names produces stupefaction from perhaps half the class, Mr. Jones expatiates: "These are places. What did the reading assignment say about them, in general. What was their relation to the French Republic?"

Most of the students write something. (The answer should be approximately that they were new countries which the French set up in areas they had conquered.) The previous night's assignment was three pages long, with a large picture on one page, but the ability to read something in the evening and to know about it the next day is one which these sophomores and juniors are still struggling to develop. They will need it in college and later on.

"Next question. What internal changes happened to the Holy Roman Empire in 1803? What basically was altered?"

Mr. Jones, slowly walking around the rows to prevent copying, reflects on his first question. Will any of these students some day find such names less strange? Will "Cisalpine" ring a bell because it reminds one of Julius Caesar's first province? It rang a bell with Mr. Smith ever since his sophomore year at a Jesuit high school, where, as part of his four years of compulsory Latin, he had marched through <u>Gallia omnia</u> with the Tenth Legion, eating the <u>frumentarium</u> and accompanying the centurions into the forest. Would "Parthenopean" ever mean anything to them? Parthenope, the legendary first name of Naples, also an opera by Handel dealing with the city's first queen. Was she a virgin, as the name indicated? Who else was called the Virgin Queen? Then "Helvetic," Caesar again, the Helvetii, his first enemies. What do modern Swiss stamps, or Swiss international license plates, say on them? The whole of Western Civilization hangs together....

"Last question: what countries were in the Third Coalition?"

When Mr. Jones had begun teaching, he had simply assigned reading each night. He thought, poor man, that his students would do it. By Thanksgiving he had realized that many of them had not opened the textbook. So he began to give unannounced reading quizzes to one or two of the Modern Europe sections

36

every day. The students disliked them so much that he knew he must be doing the right thing. Each reading quiz was worth ten points, a small amount, but the ten to fifteen which each section got each term had a powerful cumulative effect on the grade. Some students complained that they could not remember the reading even though they had done it. These were often the same students whom one could hear at supper discussing so-and-so's winning goal, which they had read about in the morning paper.

Mr. Jones collected the reading quizzes and moved to his lectern.

"Tomorrow's assignment is on the board: (1/4)183-184. I hope you don't need to ask for late lights to get it done." (Most of the next day's class would be taken up with Trafalgar and the Ulm-Austerlitz campaign, which the book dealt with summarily. There was no point in assigning reading which ran ahead of the day's class. These beginning students needed a double dose.)

"We saw yesterday how, even as Napoleon placed the Imperial crown on his head at Notre Dame on 2 December 1804, he was again at war with England—had been for over a year, since the Treaty of Amiens collapsed and William Pitt resumed office. England would never accept a France which was too strong, and just as she had implacably opposed Louis XIV in the War of the League of Augsburg and the War of the Spanish Succession, so she would oppose Napoleon. Naturally Napoleon was not content to do nothing. He was planning operations designed to force England to make peace."

"The period 1803-1805 was one of great anxiety for England. I don't like to equate Napoleon with Hitler, since that insults the former and flatters the latter, but the military situation was certainly comparable to 1940, when the Germans seemed about to invade at any time. Warning beacons were ready along the coast to signal a French landing, and the British fleet was on the alert. Most of France's ports were blockaded."

"What were the British doing diplomatically in this period?" Mr. Jones asked the class. About eight hands went up. "Anne?"

"Trying to get help?"

"Right. From whom?"

"Russia and Austria."

"Right. Now why Austria entered the war is explained in the text, but it's a little confusing. What was the Holy Roman Empire?" This time about four hands. "Trevor?"

"It was all the German countries led by Austria."

"Right." Mr. Jones went to the board. "The Holy Roman Empire consisted of two great powers, Austria and ..." He turned to the class. "Anyone."

"Prussia," said three students at once.

"Good. Then there were about half a dozen medium-sized states, with Bavaria being the largest, and around 300 small countries." This was put on the board. "The titular head of the H.R.E. was the Emperor, who was also the King of Austria. What family was this?" Lots of hands. "Paul?"

"The Hohenzollerns."

"No, that's Prussia. Heather?"

"The Hapsburgs."

"That's right. The Emperor didn't really have much power as Emperor; however, as head of the largest state he had a lot of influence. The H.R.E. was an anachronism." Mr. Jones paused, and looked at the class. "What's an anachronism?"

Only a couple of hands went up. "Remember what I said on day one: if you hear a word you don't know, ask me. A lecture isn't a sermon: you can interrupt. Joanne?"

"It's something that's not ... it's out of place in time ..." She giggled. ""I'm not sure how to put it."

"No, that's fine. Anachronism means something outdated or inappropriate for the time it's in. A Model T Ford on a modern highway is an anachronism. The Holy Roman Empire was obsolete. These dozens of little states couldn't keep their independence in a Europe dominated by great powers. In 1803 the Diet, or parliament, of the Empire passed a law which your text calls the Act of Secularization." This went on the board. "The book uses this term because the more usual German one is harder to remember. The German term for the Act of Secularization is this." Mr. Jones turned to the board and slowly wrote "Reichsdeputationshauptschluss." Several students were chuckling by the time he finished. He turned to the class. "You don't have to know this for the quiz. I include it at no extra charge. This law said that the little states would be absorbed by Prussia and the medium states. Austria would get nothing, because none of the tiny states were inside of or next to Austria. Naturally the Austrians would never let this law go into effect. Why would they want their rival Prussia to grow larger? You remember the trouble Frederick II, the Great, gave Austria when he took Silesia in 1740. But who *was* willing to support the Act of Secularization? Yes, indeed, Napoleon. Napoleon saw this as a chance to extend France's influence east of the Rhine and further weaken Austria, whom the French had already beaten twice since the revolution began—remember the Battle of Marengo and the treaties of Campo Formio and Luneville. Austria would never accept the French revolutionary government. Remember that Marie Antoinette, despite her French name, was a Hapsburg, Maria Theresa's daughter and an aunt of the now Holy Roman Emperor, Francis II. So when Napoleon appeared as a friend of the medium states and Prussia, Austria decided to go to war rather than see the Empire reorganized without her consent. Austria was also enticed by the English, of course, who were there, as usual, with their checkbook, offering aid."

Mr. Jones paused so the students, taking notes, could keep up. He was of the peripatetic school of teachers, constantly walking back and forth as he talked, never at the podium except when consulting his notes, which he did but rarely. He took a sip of water from the plastic cup on his desk in the corner.

"But what about Russia? Why did Russia become involved? Catherine the Great had died in 1796, leaving the throne to her son Paul I. Paul was another of the crazy tsars, like Peter III, Catherine's husband, whom she had overthrown and killed in 1762—you'll remember how Peter had taken Russia out of the

Seven Years War on the point of victory because of his admiration for Frederick the Great. Anyway, after five years of Paul I's eccentric behavior, many of the nobles at court were alienated and decided that the tsar had to go. He went in 1801. One night he choked to death on a scarf. Two nobles were holding the ends of the scarf at the time and pulling hard. It was quite a scene: the assassins had broken into the tsar's bedroom. Paul's eldest son Alexander succeeded his father. Alexander I was not a direct participant in the plot, as far as we know, but he made no effort to punish the murderers, who continued to hold places at court."

"The new tsar was only twenty-seven, very idealistic and well-intentioned, but very inexperienced. He was surrounded by equally naive advisors. These people told the tsar that only Russia could defeat the French Revolution. After all, had not General Suvorov beaten the French in the War of the Second Coalition, while Napoleon was in Egypt, until Paul I quarreled with the Austrians and ordered his troops home in 1799? Advised and flattered by these pinheads, Alexander came to see himself as the savior of the Old Regime. What was the Old Regime? Alan?"

"The form of government before 1789."

"Right: pre-Revolutionary Divine Right Monarchy. The tsar also was offered aid by the English, whose army was too small to oppose Napoleon. However, the main reason, or excuse, which the tsar used for going to war was not given in your book. I don't know why it was omitted, since it's famous, and it's also one of the chief crimes attributed to Napoleon. Considering that the author of your text doesn't much like the Emperor, I'm surprised he doesn't tell you about the Duke of Enghien." Mr. Jones wrote the name on the board.

"The Duke of Enghien was a relative of Louis XVI. He became an emigré and so escaped the Terror, but for some reason he settled just across the French border in the German state of Baden. French agents kept him under surveillance, and there were reports that he received many secret visitors.

Napoleon concluded that the Duke was running a spy ring and was probably planning his assassination. There had already been a couple of attempts on Napoleon's life. The Count of Artois, Louis XVI's youngest brother, whom we'll eventually meet as King Charles X, was certainly plotting against Napoleon."

"In March 1804 French troops entered Baden, arrested the Duke, and took him to Fontainebleu, outside Paris. He was in one night tried by court martial, found guilty of treason, sentenced to death, and shot."

"Napoleon was convinced that the Duke of Enghien was plotting against him, although the duke probably was not doing so. Napoleon also, we believe, wanted to show the leftists in France—the former Jacobins and radical republicans—that he would never restore the monarchy. By killing a Bourbon he obviously destroyed any chance of a reconciliation with the pretender, Louis XVIII, Louis XVI's middle brother."

"This execution, or murder if you prefer, as well as the violation of neutral territory that went with it, has earned Napoleon tremendous condemnation, both at the time and since. More ink has been spilled over the demise of this one nobleman than over the thousands of Turkish prisoners whom Napoleon had shot at Jaffa during the Egyptian Campaign, as you may recall my mentioning when we studied that. Fouché, Napoleon's police chief, himself an ex-Representative on Mission with blood on his hands from the Terror, supposedly said of the execution, 'It's worse than a crime—it's a mistake.' Certainly it alienated a lot of people outside France."

"Among those alienated was Tsar Alexander I. Remember him? We're looking at why Russia joined the Third Coalition. The tsar was terribly upset by Enghien's execution. He put his court into mourning. He said that Europe would never be safe while so terrible a man as Napoleon was alive. I've always thought it rather odd that the tsar was so mortally offended by this execution of this French nobleman but managed to tolerate the assassins of his own father so easily, without punishing them.

But, at any rate, the execution of the Duke of Enghien was a major cause of Russia's joining the latest Coalition."

By now the board was full. Mr. Jones paused to erase part of it, to make room for the next topic. With twelve minutes left in the period, he could cover part of the Trafalgar Campaign after all. Tomorrow's classes would see the Sun of Austerlitz rise again—four times, in fact—and get to the Treaty of Pressburg. Then came a film on Trafalgar, then on to Jena and Friedland and the meeting on the raft at Tilsit.

The bell rang at 9:35. Now came a ten-minute break, after which Mr. Jones would repeat the same material for a second Modern Europe section. Then he would teach the same thing again a third time. Next would come lunch, with a table of students, then yet another MEH section, the fourth and last one of the day. Sixth hour was a free period, so he could walk home and read his mail. Then finally came his Twentieth Century Europe class, fifteen seniors, today doing Hitler's early life through the Beer Hall Putsch and the writing of <u>Mein Kampf</u> (Mr. Jones had had the first period off today, and had slept until 7:45.) Last of all there would be extra help for twenty minutes or so, if anyone came in, and an hour or so of class preparation and grading. Mr. Jones was not on duty that night, so it was an easy day.

Most classes at SLA were taught by the lecture method. This statement will excite the horror of many modern educators. Lecturing has been so roundly condemned by schools of education that the very word is taboo. A whole vocabulary of scornful, pejorative phrases has been created to excoriate lecturing: "teacher telling," it's called, and it leads to "rote memorization" of "dull facts" and produces "regurgitation" on tests. Students, say the educators, must instead "discover" things, and "think for themselves." They must never just learn something because a teacher tells them to. "Discussion," is the key, a "vigorous exchange of ideas" in which students learn to "tolerate opposing viewpoints" (without, of course, ever condemning any viewpoints, all of which are equally valid as long as they are suitably liberal and politically correct.)

The master pedagogues with Ed.D. degrees also recommend, sometimes, the "Socratic method" of teaching, which proves that they have never read Plato. Socrates, despite his façade of humility, usually knew very well what he wanted his interlocutors to believe. He began by publicly humiliating them, and, after reducing them to utter self-contradictory incoherence, he told them what was what, in a "discussion" in which the student's "thinking for himself" was largely limited to a series of responses such as, "I agree. Yes. Certainly. It must be so, Socrates. Indeed. Who can doubt it?"

Lecturing is a terrible method of teaching when the lecturer doesn't know much about his subject. When a man has been hired because he has coaching certificates in two sports—and there are few public school districts which don't scrutinize a candidate's coaching ability far more closely than his teaching ability—and is then assigned to teach, say, World History, so he'll have something to do in the mornings...well, such a "teacher" should indeed eschew lecturing. When the biology teacher has not read a biology book since receiving his B.A., and his mind is awhirl with what sort of strategy his team will employ in the evening's Big Game, he will not be much good as a lecturer. No, indeed. Better to give the students busy work, or start a discussion where the blind can lead the blind.

But if the teaching is done by a scholar, by someone who is in a classroom—not just working at a school, but <u>in a classroom</u>—because he <u>wants</u> to be there, by the sort of eccentric who is possessed by his subject as a saint is possessed by a god, by a <u>teacher</u>, someone who (with apologies to Oliver Cromwell) knows what he fights for and loves what he knows ....well, then, a lecture, which is the simplification of a complex subject by a mature, well-stocked, and thoughtful mind, and its presentation in a logical and entertaining way, is a fine teaching method.

Because so many "educators" are not trained, or too lazy, or afraid, to <u>teach</u>, to <u>impart</u> <u>knowledge</u> which they <u>know</u> the

43

students should <u>learn</u>, we have college graduates who can't find Hungary on a map, or name the author of The Scarlet Letter (never mind summarizing its plot), who can't solve an equation with one unknown or place the Civil War within fifty years of its occurrence.

XII. PARENTS

The school year was divided into three terms. Fall Term classes ended the first week of November and were followed by three days of final exams and a brief vacation so that teachers would have time to grade their finals and write their comments. Comment writing was a major activity at SLA, as it is at any independent school. Whenever a student failed a test, the teacher filled out an "academic warning slip" (usually called a flunk slip), using a four-copy NCR form. (One copy went to the student's parents, one to his advisor, one into his file, and the fourth was thrown away.) Five weeks into the term came midterm comments, required for students who were doing poorly. At the end of each term teachers wrote full comments on all students. There was also a Commendation Form for students who improved during the term.

This writing was a lot of work, especially the term comments, which were written right after grading a pile of final exams. To grade, say, seventy blue books, each with a long essay and many shorter parts, and then write seventy individual comments, certainly took the edge off of a week's vacation. However, comment-writing is an art which, once mastered, becomes fairly easy. After all, most students fell into groups or types, and similar comments could be used for each category. One praised the A and B students and exhorted them to keep up the good work; the C students were told to work harder; the D and F students were chastised, and their individual faults catalogued. For instance:

This term we studied the period 1517-1790, including the Reformation, Stuart England, the Age of Absolutism (with special attention to the Sun King), and the origins and opening events of the French Revolution.

45

Barbara failed the two hour tests (48, 57), three of four quizzes, and eight of ten reading quizzes. She earned a 61 on the final, not enough to raise her failing grade to a passing one. Barbara must take more notes in class, do the daily assignments with scrupulous care, and make use of extra help regularly.

Comments sometimes employed euphemisms, such as "has difficulty in distinguishing historical figures" for the boy who confused Luther with Henry VIII, or "could apply herself more" for the girl with ten unexcused absences, but by and large the comments were written clearly and forcefully. There was not much use of educational jargon because most of the SLA teachers, who did not need state certification in order to teach, had taken few or no education courses. Indeed, that is one reason why most were effective teachers.

The weekend after the fall midterm grades came out was Parents' Weekend. Mothers and fathers were encouraged to come to the school to see what they were paying for. Friday classes were shortened to allow for an afternoon pep rally, there was a concert Friday night, the sports teams all played home games, the college counsellors held a meeting for parents of juniors and seniors, etc.

But the main events of Parents' Weekend were the teacher conferences, for two hours on Friday afternoon and three on Saturday morning. These were held in the gym, where the teachers sat at card tables and the parents lined up to speak with them.

These conferences were quite a physical ordeal for teachers with a lot of students. About two-thirds of the parents did show up, many from far away, and this meant that a teacher might spend over five solid hours sitting on a flimsy folding chair and talking with couple after couple for five or six minutes each. The veteran faculty took occasional breaks, simply excusing themselves for a few minutes even if there was a big line. (It was best to do this when the parents of an A student sat down, for they were sure to be in a good mood.) Those masochists who never interrupted their conferences finished with headaches and bladder problems, as well as discovering, when they finally stood up to go, that the folding chairs had cut off the circulation in their lower legs.

The meetings themselves were usually painless. Here is one area where public school teachers might envy their private school counterparts. Public school faculty are sitting targets for every disgruntled, overprotective, and/or crazy parent in their district. There are many parents today who harass teachers, and who don't hesitate to blame the school when any problems arise. This is not usually the case at private schools. Oh, there are occasionally cranks and crackpots—indeed, one oft-heard comment among teachers is that they better understand why a student is so nutty after meeting the people who engendered him—but by and large, at SLA, parents were so grateful, so deeply grateful, that the school was willing not only to educate their kids but to feed them, house them, and bring them up, that they could only smile with glee, listen carefully to what each teacher said, and promise to cooperate in every way.

It might seem odd that parents paying a fortune to a private school would be less critical and vociferous than those who were paying nothing (directly) to a public school, but there were reasons for this anomaly. SLA did indeed give a good education to those students who worked, and was pretty good at motivating them to work. But, beyond this, was the simple fact that, if worse came to worst, if push came to shove, if a parent complained too much, SLA could....could....invoke the ultimate sanction....impose the supreme penalty....and....send the kid home. And the thought that the school might pull the trigger and ship junior home again was enough to give even the most critical parents pause.

When all is said and done, a private school's decisive advantage over a public school is the ability to throw students out quickly. SLA exercised that power reluctantly and quite rarely, but it was there, like a nuclear deterrent. The druggies, drinkers, and bullies admitted by accident could be terminated at any time, and the morons and the fatally lazy were reviewed at the end of each term. Students were not "promoted" at SLA, they were "invited back." Withholding a contract was a powerful tool to motivate most borderline students.

XIII. DE GUSTIBUS / DISGUSTIBUS

The most senior member of the staff at SLA was Otto Auswurf, who had been at the school for an astonishing forty-one years. Otto was fifty-nine. He had come to SLA just after World War II, a young man almost unemployable, for he had not finished high school and was barely literate. But St. Lawrence had a place for him; he found a home there; he never left. He was a fixture at SLA, and the graduates certainly remembered him. Most could not have forgotten him had they tried, for, when confronted in a restaurant with some badly-cooked meat, when beset with indigestion from a treacherous pie, when, dyspeptic and insomniac, they thrashed about in bed because of a little botulism in the fish sauce, they thought of Otto and they muttered, "Well, it could be worse."

Otto Auswurf was the Food Service Manager. He had risen to that height, which gave him control of a large kitchen and seventeen employees, through decades of faithful service to the Bonne Cuisine Corporation, a big food supply company which numbered SLA among its accounts. Otto had started out as an assistant dishwasher, and as he learned the trade he moved up the alimentary hierarchy: associate dishwasher, senior dishwasher, assistant cook, pastry cook, chief cook, manager. But, despite scaling these heights, he remained, in his heart of hearts, an assistant dishwasher, and his knowledge of nutrition could have been engraved on the head of a pin with lots of room left over. As for variety of foods and new creations, Otto was totally insensitive. He was like an ancient Roman: the <u>mos maiorum</u>, the ways of the ancestors, were all he would ever need to guide him.

There were, for example, five breakfast menus at SLA, one for each school day. (On weekends, when few got up early, just cereal and toast were available.) Each was served on the same day of the week. This was of some help to those faculty and

49

students who had trouble getting started in the mornings, because such people were at least assured, if they went to breakfast, of knowing what day it was. If they ate pancakes, it was Tuesday.

The promotional material of Bonne Cuisine assured its clients that all of its menus were prepared by skilled dietitians whose every waking moment was devoted to sedulous concern for their clients' health and happiness. This would have come as a surprise to the people at SLA, however. Anyone with even a modicum of nutritional knowledge, or just common sense, knew darn well that their chances of longevity diminished with every meal they ate in the refectory. (Public schools have cafeterias. Private schools have refectories. Medieval monasteries had refectories, too, but their food was better.)

Every entree was fried to within an inch of its life. The egg was the staple breakfast food. Relatively harmless things, like hot dogs, were embalmed in grease. On Monday the breakfast was scrambled eggs thickly coated with melted cheese. On Wednesdays one was regaled with a fried egg, a slice of fried ham, and a slice of cheese on a toasted roll. This thing was called "Breakfast on a Bun," but it should have been called the Heart Attack Special.

Otto Auswurf, who couldn't spell "cholesterol," provided SLA with an endless array of incredibly awful meals. There were stews whose contents were unidentifiable by any means short of a forensics laboratory, pieces of meat whose original source it was better not to know, and puddings which, if not immediately eaten, set like cement and could be used as hockey pucks. There was a ham salad whose very smell caused men to weep and women to faint. There were deeds done in the cauldrons of the St. Lawrence kitchen which would have brought a blush of shame to the three witches in <u>Macbeth</u>. The famous black broth of ancient Sparta was tasty and refreshing compared with Otto Auswurf's soups, and the sailors of the Royal Navy in Nelson's day had enjoyed better biscuits.

One of Otto Auswurf's salient characteristics was his utter indifference to popular opinion. It did not make the slightest difference to him if people ate what he served or not. On those rare occasions when some dish was well-received and the student waiters wanted seconds for their tables, the kitchen would immediately run out, and it would not be served with any more frequency than before. On the other hand, when whole bowls or platters of some noisome refuse came back untouched, often with the plastic wrap still intact, Otto would put them in the freezer and serve them again next week. Middle-aged alumni could return to SLA and, at lunch time, feel as if they had never left, since the food being served was identical to what they remembered having eaten twenty years before. Indeed, it may have been the same food. One amazing, but true, story about the "durability" of food at SLA concerned the rolls occasionally served at Sunday dinner. A student had opened one a bit and put inside it a slip of paper with the day's date on it, then returned it to the basket. Two weeks later, at another table, another student had found the note inside the roll.

To teach and work all morning, to come down to the big refectory and sit down, hungry, and then to be served "turkey" which came in loaves wrapped in tinfoil, turkey whose slices were not "white" or "dark" but uniformly gray, synthetic potatoes apparently made of spun cotton, and brown lettuce, was a little depressing. It did not help, either, that many of the items had names which seemed highly inappropriate and unrealistic. There was "Delightful Rice" and "Pudding in a Cloud." Since the former was incredible and the latter was inedible, one had to assume that the names had been chosen euphemistically, or perhaps were apotropaic, i.e., chosen to avert harm, as the Greeks called the Furies the "Kindly Ones."

Otto Auswurf had such seniority and authority that firing him was unthinkable. He had made his kitchen an autonomous fiefdom and he could rest secure in his job as long as he liked. Or so he thought. All unknown and unsuspected, opposition to his mad reign was building. Not forever could this arrogant and ignorant man continue with impunity to nauseate his victims. The day of reckoning was approaching!

XIV. DEVELOPMENTS IN DEVELOPMENT

One day in mid-October Mario Pestalozzi had visitors: three men who introduced themselves as "consultants from Chicago" when they arrived at the school. They were closeted with Mario for a long time, and then they left.

"Gee," said Mary Coster to John Fordiss, "those guys looked pretty rough. I never saw consultants with scars on their faces like that, and one was missing part of an ear."

"Yes, but they must be cultured men," replied young John, "because they were all carrying violin cases. I wonder if they'll solve our problems?"

The next day Mario held a meeting with his staff. "I tell you, kids, we're on the way to great things. The Headmaster has agreed to hire the gentlemen you saw yesterday to help us motivate major givers. Mr. Bontucci in Chicago is coordinating this effort, and we hope to expand it into a Capital Campaign that actually works. The men who were here—Mr. Garbandoni, Mr. Ricci, and Mr. Mazzarucci—will be in California working on, I mean working with, some of our more stubborn potential donors—starting with that <u>pazzo</u>, that, that <u>sciagurato</u>...well, I mean Mr. Hobart."

"Do you think they'll be able to persuade him not to give all his money to the Rosicrucians?" asked John.

"They're very good at persuasion," replied Mario with a big grin. "In fact, they're gonna make him an offer he can't refuse."

****

In the next three weeks the SLA Development Department entered a new era. The most amazing things happened, one after another. First came news that the unstable Mr. Hobart had abjured the Rosy Cross and agreed to will his entire fortune to SLA. Then two elderly alumnae, maiden ladies, sent checks for

$100,000 with fervent promises of more to come. After that the aged donut mogul, Anselm Flickermacher, for whose oft-promised "big bucks" the school had been patiently waiting for almost two decades, departed this life most unexpectedly. One day his devoted nurse called to say she could not take him for his daily excursion, but that a friend of hers would come instead. And while this friend, who was a large, powerful man named Mr. Ricci, was pushing the old man's wheelchair, he unfortunately lost control of it atop one of San Francisco's many hills. The unlucky nonagenarian began rolling down the street at an increasing rate of speed until his wheelchair stopped abruptly when it hit a curb. Obeying Newton's First Law, Mr. Flickermacher did not stop, but was precipitated from his seat and through the plate-glass window of a jewelry store. His will left SLA a million dollars, and the same amount to his faithful nurse, who immediately moved to Palermo. SLA held a nice memorial service.

Mr. Pestalozzi told his staff to make lists of all alumni who had not contributed to the Annual Fund. "We're going to amplify the Phonathon this year, folks," he said. "Anyone with any dough who doesn't give will get a personal visit from our consultants."

XV. MENS INSANA IN CORPORE SANO

The hockey season had begun on August 27, which also was the first day of school. (Now that SLA was free of the trammels imposed by the State High School League the hockey team was free to do as it liked; formerly, practice could not begin until November 15.) The team had two practices each day. The first was from six to seven-thirty A.M., which insured that the players would be exhausted when they went to class. The second was from four to six P.M., which insured they would be too tired to study well at night. As more teams were added, Lance Vance planned to have them practice throughout the day, so that a student on, say, the Dwarf Orange team would attend classes during periods one and two, then go to the arena for practice during periods three and four, then go to lunch and resume his classes in the afternoon.

When the hockey players were not on the ice they could usually be found in the weight room. This room, really a coliseum, was magnificent, newly-equipped with every device known to physical education. And this was money well-spent, for the weight room got far more use than did the library. Everyone needs to take pride in himself, and since the average serious hockey player learns quite early in life, around age twelve in fact, that no one is ever going to admire him for his incisive wit or brilliant mind, he had better go into body-building.

The results were certainly remarkable. There were sixteen-year-old boys at SLA who looked like advertisements for Gold's Gym. They had thick, corded necks, bulging arms, barrel chests, huge calves, and whenever possible they wore shorts and cut-off T-shirts to display their sinews. The corridors and classrooms of SLA sometimes looked like an anthropological living history museum, where homo sapiens could meet his ancestors still walking around. If you had removed the modern clothing from

Bruto Grubnecker, the hockey captain, and given him a loincloth, you would have realized that the Piltdown Man was not a hoax after all. One day Mr. Jones, watching one of the players go by in profile, had an eerie and unsettling feeling, for, gazing at those bulging muscles, that prognathous jaw, those slightly recessed eyes, and that flat cranium above a minuscule forehead, the teacher knew that SLA had enrolled the Missing Link. Mr. Jones wondered if dissecting a champion hockey player would reveal an anatomy similar to that of a stegosaurus or a triceratops: i.e., a vestigial brain or nerve complex at the base of the spine which controlled the legs, a task which the tiny brain far away in the head was too weak to manage.

This pursuit of Herculean physiques led to more serious problems than unsightly teenagers. It was inevitable that some boys would get into steroids and bring the drugs back to school. This offered as good an explanation as any for the disturbing incident the previous April, when a junior had pulled a knife on the Dean of Students and held him at bay in a dorm room for half an hour while threatening to kill him. By the time the police arrived the boy had been talked into surrendering his formidable poignard, but the whole affair was thought to be a little unsettling. One did not expect it at St. Lawrence Academy. It was not at all refined—it seemed very "public school." The boy was of course dismissed, and rumor had it that "roid rage" had been the cause of his temporary insanity.

Such a trivial contretemps, however, was all part of building a winning sport. Coach Vance was busy throughout the fall drilling his little Neanderthals into a gang of truly brutal thugs. They had <u>spirit</u>, they had <u>pride</u>, they went about with their heads held high. They terrorized the weaker boys in the dorms and clearly considered themselves the Master Race. They were "gonna kick ass" when the games began.

It was this hubris, combined with their innate stupidity, which had led the veteran players to devise a very distinctive initiation for the first-year team members. One night Joe Spofford, a housemaster on duty in the boys' dorm, became

55

worried that something was seriously wrong on the third floor. His concern was caused not by a lot of noise, but by a lot of silence. Between 10 P.M., when study hall ended, and 10:45, the time for lights out on school nights, there was normally quite an uproar in the dorm, but Mr. Spofford was aware of an ominous hush at the west end of the third-floor corridor. Being a conscientious man, he went down the corridor to see what was up, and he heard murmurs coming from one room. This room seemed to be full of people. Mr. Spofford decided not to knock: he just used his master key and went in.

There were about fifteen boys, all hockey players, in the small room. Two of them were holding down a freshman teammate, who was naked and spread-eagled on the floor. A third boy was spraying shaving cream on the freshman's middle, preparatory to the shaving about to be administered by a senior, who held a straight razor in his hand.

The boys were dismayed by their housemaster's abrupt advent. They stared at him aghast, and finally one said, "Oh, hi, Mr. Spofford. We're just initiating Mike here into the team. You know, it's a fun thing we do."

Joe Spofford, 26, M.A. in English, in his second year of teaching, closed his eyes briefly and realized how right his parents had been when they had advised him to go to law school. "Actually, I didn't know," he said. "Everybody out. Go to your rooms. Mike, go take a shower. Jim, give me the razor. I expect that the Dean will want to talk to most of you tomorrow."

The boys shuffled out. Mike Stang, the victim, whose room it was, said, "Gee, Mr. Spofford, I hope I don't get in trouble for this," as he hastily rose and wrapped a towel around himself.

"Why would <u>you</u> get in trouble?" asked the teacher.

"I mean with the team. The older guys already shaved all the other newbies. I don't want to be ostracized."

Mr. Spofford looked at the boy. "Mike, just go wash up. And if you can use a word like 'ostracized,' you might want to consider if you really belong on a hockey team."

The repercussions of this incident were that Lance Vance delivered a stern rebuke to his team. He told them that they must not behave that way any more. He forbade them to shave the body hair off fellow players. Two boys were prohibited from playing in the next game. The Dean, who felt that the matter was far more serious and should have led to suspensions and probations, was overruled by the Headmaster, to whom Lance Vance had spoken and whom he persuaded to let him, the coach, handle the situation.

The next hockey game was against Oakton. SLA won a great victory, defeating their opponents 5-1. Oakton was fifty-five miles from Vacheville. The game ended at 9:15, and the team returned at 11:35. The next day, six sophomore players failed a Modern Europe test, three juniors failed an English vocab. quiz, and none of the seniors turned in their math homework.

XVI. "THANK GOD I HAVE DONE MY DUTY" (LORD NELSON)

The faculty members who did not live in dormitories constituted the group known as "duty masters." Each school day one was on duty, while on weekends a team of three handled any chaperoning for which volunteers could not be found, supervised detention and work squads, and kept an eye on Laud Hall.

Weekday duty began at 5:30 PM, when the duty master arrived in the refectory at the start of dinner. He remained until the meal was over at 7:00. (Lunches were sit-down, but suppers were buffet.) During this time he supervised the meal, prevented rowdiness, quelled incipient food fights, and tried to make sure that students cleared their places and made no messes. From 7 to 8 he patrolled Laud Hall, serving as the "adult presence" which is so necessary to prevent liability suits. He periodically checked the answering machine in the faculty lounge—or he would have, had that machine not been broken for over two years. (No duty master had ever reported its breakdown, since its non-functionality slightly reduced the work load.) From 8:00 to 10:00 he was in charge of Evening Supervised Study Hall (ESSH).

ESSH was a form of punishment. Each week teachers and houseparents submitted to the Academic Office names of students who weren't turning their work in, who abused their dormitory study time (which was also 8:00 to 10:00) by being out of their rooms or noisy, or who just weren't applying themselves enough. The weekly list was published, and the students on it would spend their two hours of compulsory study time sitting at a desk in a big room under the stern eye of the Duty Master: no talking, no walking, no tunes, no food, no comfy chairs: just a desk and schoolbooks.

This was a good system. Since the students loathed ESSH, its mere existence made many work just to keep out of it. It removed from dorms people who interfered with those who actually did study. Since it lasted just five class days at a time, it encouraged those in it with the hope of soon meriting release.

It also gave the Duty Master the worst job in the school. Dormparents were worse off on the whole, because they did one-in-three duty and had to live with the students, but for sheer concentrated misery ESSH could exceed anything else at SLA.

The problem, of course, was that it put some of the worst elements in the school in one room for a long time. Sometimes it was not too bad. If a substantial number of the inmates had a big test the next day, or if the study hall was small, say six or seven, the time could pass without excessive stress. But one could never tell. Every study hall was different, even with the same group on different nights. Some chemistry, some subtle and invisible aura, determined the ambiance of each ESSH. Trouble might start with students trying to sit in seats other than the ones assigned on the chart and complaining when they weren't allowed to. Sometimes students came in late, or noisily, or with no books or pens. On bad nights the restlessness would not die down. Someone would get up without permission, someone would have smuggled in a Walkman or a can of pop, someone would drop a heavy book.

The Duty Master, seated at the big desk, had the choice of watching the room with hawk-like vigilance, which assured he got none of his own work done, or of trying to read, write tests, or grade papers while intermittently inspecting the room (which was large, with sixty desks, although ESSH rarely went above twenty-five students.) Since any adult of normal intelligence would go mad if he stared at a room for two hours, and nobody at SLA could waste that much time anyway, ESSH always presented the challenge of trying to do two things at once.

Mr. Jones, the European History teacher, had a philosophical view of it all. He knew that in supervising ESSH he was taking part in a great private-school tradition, a tradition imported (like the seating in chapel) from England. This was "prep," this was "great hall," this was "invigilated study." This was where Evelyn Waugh's Mr. Pennyfeather was drunk and caned twenty-three boys. It was where Mr. Chips had given several hundred lines to the boy who had dropped his desk top.

And that, thought Mr. Jones, was the problem: in modern America one could not "cane" students or give them "lines." The study halls remained, but the use of force or laboriously wasted time were gone. Nor could one get away with going there drunk, although that might have helped. Today one depended on voice alone. (Of course there was detention, but the people who were in ESSH were usually in detention every week anyway. Detention met from 7:00 to 9:00 on Fridays. It was held in the same room. It was, in fact, identical to ESSH.)

After the first hour of ESSH it was customary to take a short break. This was unfortunate, because it tended to destroy whatever quiet had been achieved. Students would return late. Sometimes fights would erupt between rivals, or some pariah would be picked on while the Duty Master was out of the room. But a break was needed, since human bladders can stand only so much strain, and the Duty Master, who was responsible for the whole of Laud Hall, had to glance at the rest of the building. Still, it was disturbing to return to the room to find that a student had thrown someone else's books out of the (second-story) window.

Mr. Jones often felt like throwing some of the students out of the window, or hitting them with a stick. But he couldn't do that. He had also learned early in his career that losing his temper was always a mistake. It made him feel awful afterwards. So he managed his study halls with a mixture of sternness, cajolery, and humor. When these failed, he had recourse to the ultimate weapon in a modern teacher's arsenal: sarcasm.

Most adolescents have extremely fragile and sensitive egos. Even more than adults they hate to be embarrassed before their peers, to be singled out or made fun of. Teachers know this and therefore refrain from doing these things to their charges, lest they scar their psyches, mangle their ids, and turn them into maladjusted and dysfunctional adults. But sometimes the kids really ask for it. Much of the indiscipline in a class or a study hall occurs to annoy or to anger a teacher, to get a rise out of him. There are some young people who have teacher-baiting as a hobby, and although the percentage of such miscreants was smaller at SLA than at a public school, because such types usually got themselves thrown out for some serious infraction, they were there, especially at the start of the year.

Mr. Jones saw no reason to play into the hands of these malicious imps, and had concluded long ago that the best thing to do when confronted by a really bad case was to turn the tables on the would-be tormentor. If the wretch was trying to get his fellows to laugh at the teacher, well, give him a taste of his own medicine. While the sword of sarcasm was usually left in its scabbard, there was a time for it to flash in defense of discipline and respect. Mr. Jones did not mind the risk of scarring someone for life or turning him into a Charlie Manson if it would make his own life a little easier.

On one occasion, when an obnoxious student seated in the rear row was amusing himself by repeatedly banging the back of his head against the wall, Mr. Jones just told him to stop before he damaged the wall. So simple-minded a joke had succeeded very well in getting a class of fifteen-year-olds to laugh at the head-banger. Another time a plump young woman had come in quite late, ostentatiously dropped her book bag on the floor with a loud thump, and then, having some difficulty in getting into her seat, interrupted things still further by exclaiming, "I hate these mini-desks."

Mr. Jones looked at her and said, "Mini-desks? Maybe it's the maxi-you." The study hall completely broke up and Jane never came late again (although, if looks could kill, Mr. Jones would have left in a stretcher.)

Tonight, in mid-October, the study hall was not large, just twelve, but most of the inmates were freshmen. Ninth-grade boys tend to be more obnoxious than older students in the petty ways that disrupt civilized assemblies. Usually it is during the summer of their fifteenth year that boys develop vestiges of maturity and become capable of doing things like sitting still, paying attention for more than five minutes at a time, and refraining from hitting each other for no discernible reasons. (Girls, who are much easier to teach than boys, rarely have these obnoxious traits to overcome.) Mr. Jones did not teach freshmen and so did not know most of these students.

The study hall was quiet for the first half hour or so, and Mr. Jones was busy grading quizzes. Then some people started whispering and had to be reprimanded, then one boy opened a can of Pepsi, which Mr. Jones confiscated, and then someone loudly broke wind.

Breaking wind has a never-failing effect on the risibility of teenagers (and some adults), and there is nothing like a good loud fart to sew discord in a classroom or study hall. This particular explosion sounded, in that large and largely empty room, like something produced by Emile Zola's character, Jesus Christ, in his novel La Terre. Mr. Jones looked up in great annoyance. Giggles and cries of "phew" were beginning. It was obvious that the perpetrator was the little runt three seats back in the middle row, who, seeing Mr. Jones glaring at him, said sweetly, "I passed gas."

"Well, that's about the only thing you've ever passed around here, isn't it?" rasped the teacher. "Maybe if you studied you could pass a course. Now get to work!"

As things returned to normal Mr. Jones recalled other nights, other study halls. There had been the time that a student had brought with him a copy of Playboy and Mr. Jones looked up just as he was displaying the centerfold to the boy seated behind him. Mr. Jones had slowly gotten up and slowly walked towards the young man, who frantically folded up Miss November and tossed the magazine next to his neighbor's desk. When Mr. Jones arrived the first boy said, idiotically, "It's his," and the second said angrily, "It's yours." Mr. Jones smiled, picked up the magazine, said, "Now, it's mine," and returned to his desk.

One time things had seemed very serious. In a crowded and quite unruly study hall a huge junior had suddenly jumped up, yelled, "You hit me," to a boy seated some distance away, run over to him, slapped him across the face, and then half lifted him out of his desk with one hand while clenching his fist for the estocado. Mr. Jones watched this in growing alarm, thinking he was about to witness a murder and wondering if he should lock himself in a side room, for if this student, Rufus King, had really flipped, he could certainly have cleaned out the whole study hall. But duty called, and Mr. Jones found himself rushing towards the berserk behemoth, putting a hand on his shoulder, and saying, "Rufus, don't." (He sincerely hoped that Rufus wouldn't, since there wasn't much he could do if Rufus did.) And Rufus didn't. Restrained by some vestige of reason or respect, he withheld his fist from his trembling victim's face, then let him go and allowed himself to be walked back to his desk, muttering curses and obscenities. Another boy, who knew Rufus well, came over to help calm him down. Mr. Jones told Rufus he could return at once to his dorm room, and was relieved when the boy left.

By then, of course, the whole study hall, unruly a few moments before, had become as silent as a tomb, and stayed that way until it ended. (It turned out that Rufus had been hit on the ear with a spitball and that this had triggered his manifestation of the rage and frustration which had been building up inside him during his academically unsuccessful time at SLA. He left later in the year.)

The Duty Master carried with him a folder, the "Duty Master Log," which contained all sorts of helpful information. There was, for example, a sheet telling what to do if you found a dead student. (Notify the Headmaster or the Dean, who will convene the Crisis Committee—nine members were listed—to handle the emergency; dial 911; don't talk to any reporters.) There was a sheet on how to use the telephone to contact the night guard's beeper, a procedure so complicated that no one had ever used it successfully. There was a six-page blurb called "The Warning Signs of Suicide." This was of recent vintage, suicide being "in" as a hot topic. (The previous year the trendy subject had been "drug abuse indicators." Next year it would be "conflict resolution." The faculty would get very worked up about each year's topic, hold meetings, form committees, pass resolutions, argue, worry, feel guilty ... then summer vacation would intervene and by the fall the previous year's crucial topic would have vanished like an autumn leaf, leaving behind no discernible changes.)

Mr. Jones enjoyed reading the suicide document because it was a valuable form of professional development and taught him a lot. At the top of the very first page, for example, it said:

I. VERBAL WARNING SIGNS
    A. Has spoken directly of suicide. Blatant statements about ending their (sic) life, such as:
       - "I'm going to kill myself"
       - "I want to die."

Mr. Jones was grateful for this insight. Further on he learned that "Suicide is an emotional erosion. The decision to take one's life does not happen spontaneously. Suicide happens after a series of crises and stressful events..." and that "a move to a new neighborhood" or "loss of a romantic relationship" were among the "crises and stressful events which may occur during adolescence." How enlightening! Among the "Behavioral Warning Signs" of suicide were "making out a will or suddenly reconciling with long-time enemies." Poor Mr. Jones had thought that the former was a sign of prudence, and the latter one of charity. But apparently almost anything could be a suicide warning, and the document was rather confusing when it listed, as other omens of impending self-destruction, "eating too little or too much," "a desire for punishment," "a desire to avoid punishment," and "sleeping too extensively or insomnia." Well,

well, this was all very useful, of course. Mr. Jones estimated that he had at least three suicidal symptoms, and so did all his friends and colleagues, judging from this list. Then he came to this: "A person dwelling on the topic of the hereafter or life after death could be thinking about death." Mr. Jones sighed. What did this gibberish mean? Someone "dwelling on life after death" was indeed thinking about death, wasn't he? But by this standard, was not the whole human race suicidal? The greatest philosophers, the most revered religious leaders—didn't they "dwell on the topic of the hereafter?"

Finally Mr. Jones came to the real kicker:

III. SITUATIONAL WARNING SIGNS
.....
C. 3. Is NOT currently LIVING AT HOME.

Mr. Jones began to laugh, disturbing his own study hall. Here it was in black and white: the whole SLA boarding population was at a higher risk of suicide. It was good to know.

Mr. Jones put away the blurb, thinking that it, like the endless reams of paper on similar topics which he and his colleagues received each year, was typical of the rubbish churned out for distribution to teachers by the sort of parasites on the educational profession who earned large salaries by scribbling in comfortable offices without ever teaching a class or running a study hall or dorm. Surely the world would be a nicer place if these people could be treated as Nero had treated some of the early Christians?*

There had actually been one student suicide in recent years, but that student had had the decency to shoot himself at home, during a vacation. The impact of this sad event on the school was thus minimized, and chiefly manifested itself among the

---

* cf. Tacitus, <u>Annals</u>, XV, 44

deceased's peers by their efforts to get his dorm room, which was a nice single. There was also a story that, many years back, a new teacher, on his first night of dorm duty, entered a room for bed check to find a student dangling from a noose tied to the ceiling light. But that was probably just a legend, like the ghosts in Laud Hall or the student who had sold all the baseball equipment to the townies. The dormitory light fixtures were far too flimsy to support a human body.

Also in the Duty Master Log, along with dorm housing lists, phone numbers, and weekend activity information, was the "Duty Master Report Sheet," where, each day. the "Comments/Concerns/Problems" and "Items Deserving Immediate Attention" could be written down for the Dean to know. Usually this sheet was used merely for recording absences from ESSH, broken windows, unlocked doors, and the like, but occasionally a teacher would be moved to record at length some incident and to express his thoughts and feelings. Mr. Jones still had a photocopy of his own favorite, which he had been inspired to type out late one night some years before:

This study hall went much better than last week's, but (a) half of them had my 'big quiz' tomorrow (which is not entirely coincidental) and (b) a couple of 'key people' were absent. I should note that Gary Price was somewhat troublesome until God struck him down (see below) and that Ron Larson, although essentially a harmless simpleton or child of nature, is certainly hyperactive. He cannot stay in his seat for two hours. Or one hour. Or ten minutes.

At the end of the ten-minute break, during which I had remained in the study hall, I went to the top of the stairs to call the malingerers back in, and some students said I should come down because Gary Price had fallen and struck his head. I walked down to find Price in a somewhat woozy and dazed condition sitting on one of the chairs in the corridor, and, making inquiries, was told that he felt light-headed, dizzy, and, as he summed it up, like he was high. (I did not ask him how he knew what being high felt like.) I went to call the nurse, whose line was busy, and then returned and asked Stacy Dent, who had remained with Gary, to go to the nurse's house and get her while I returned to the study hall before chaos began to reign. About fifteen minutes later I went downstairs to find Price, Dent, and the nurse in the infirmary office; Paula (the nurse) was writing out a set of instructions for Price's housemaster and roommate to the effect that if later on Price felt dizzy, or sleepy, or a number of other things, someone was to call Paula; but Paula said she felt there was no damage of a permanent nature. I gallantly offered to excuse Price from the rest of study hall, but Paula said she wanted him to 'be around people' and that he should go back to ESSH. So he did; and during the remaining half hour he seemed OK, if much more subdued than usual. When the study hall ended I gave him the note and carefully instructed him to show it to his housemaster and to call the nurse if he felt the least unwell in the course of the evening.

Price's fall was caused by some horseplay during the break in which he, having slapped Stacy, was being chased by her; he slipped and fell in the corridor outside the refectory, and the 'skid marks' can be clearly seen on the floor there.

I cannot describe my own emotions at seeing this obstreperous twerp so condignly struck down by Providence and thus rendered incapable of further disrupting my study hall, but it just goes to show that maybe there is a God.

XVII. THEOLOGY

Father Clovenhoof lived in a small cottage diagonally across from the chapel. It was hard to say if this cottage had actually been built by an architect or had been randomly assembled by spastic chimpanzees. Each window was of a slightly different size than the others, so if the screens and storm windows were not labelled—and they weren't—getting ready for summer and winter was like working on a jigsaw puzzle, with very large pieces. The front and rear sections of the house were separated by a corridor eleven feet long and twenty-nine inches wide, and, since there was only one entrance door, moving furniture into the rear rooms presented challenges similar to those of putting a ship in a bottle.

The cottage had apparently been built when electricity was still something of a novelty. There was one hideous overhead light in each room, operated by a pull-chain, and there were few electrical outlets. Or, rather, one room had four, another had one, and the bathroom had none at all. Indeed, the house had been built without a bathroom, and eventually one had been tacked on, like a shed, to the side of the house, next to the kitchen. The tub was located, somewhat unusually, under the large bathroom window, and the bathroom was on the north side of the house, insuring refreshingly cool showers in the winter. There was one closet, in the kitchen next to the refrigerator. The color scheme was white. Everything except the floors was white: the walls, the ceilings, the doors and doorknobs. (Ten years before, the then business manager, Mr. Wilson, had gotten a wonderful deal on 6,000 gallons of white paint. By now almost every campus house was done in "Wilson white," and since about 1,800 gallons of the stuff still remained, SLA faced a monochrome future for years to come.) This paint had been applied directly over wallpaper, wallpaper which in its turn had been applied over paint, which had gone on over wallpaper... If it were ever decided to finish the house properly, the services of an archaeologist might be needed, as the scraping of the walls would resemble the excavation of the levels of Troy.

The house, whose official name was East Cottage, boasted one of the finest collections of fauna in the region. Centipedes were especially abundant, and there was a profusion of flies, several species of spiders, lots of Daddy Longlegs, millipedes, ladybugs, and a sort of inchworm which could hop like a tiny kangaroo. There were, however, no cockroaches. The centipedes had eaten them all.

North Cottage was heated, from time to time, by a gas furnace which belonged in the Smithsonian. When it came on, the "water knock" sounded like the Cannonade of Valmy, and the floor actually vibrated. This furnace regularly, and mysteriously, ran out of water, usually about two A.M. during cold waves. Since the dirt-floored cellar was accessible only from outside the house, the lucky inhabitant often faced the excitement of leaping out of bed in a forty-degree room, throwing a heavy coat over his pajamas, exchanging his slippers for boots, going out into six or eight inches of snow and permafrost, forcing his way into the dark cellar through the misshapen wooden door, running some water into the boiler, racing back to bed and waiting an hour until the house had warmed up to sixty, or even sixty-five.

Father Clovenhoof found his cottage acceptable despite its limitations. The front part could be left open for visitors while the rear could be used for his private studies. One evening the cleric was sitting in one of the three rear rooms at a big old desk, examining a large volume, a reprint by the Thoth Publishing House of a sixteenth-century commentary on the Kabala, when the doorbell rang. Fr. Clovenhoof got up, locked the room, and went to the door to admit Lance Vance.

The chaplain, greatly surprised to see who was visiting him, sat the hockey coach down on an old sofa and asked what he could do for him. Lance said, "Well, ya know, padre, tomorrow's our Big Game." Fr. Clovenhoof nodded, although in fact this important piece of information had somehow slipped his mind. "Well, padre, me and the boys was wonderin' if you could maybe meet with us in chapel before the game, you know, and say a prayer for us. Sorta appeal for a good game, and everyone doing their best. The boys'd like that and I think it'd help 'em play real good."

Asmodeus Clovenhoof looked in astonishment at the beefy coach. His initial reaction was to snort and ask if Mr. Vance thought that Heaven cared a rap about a hockey game. But then he realized that while the coach's request might, to an ordinary man, appear ridiculous or even blasphemous, to a mind deranged by athletic mania it was perfectly reasonable. After all, thought Fr. Clovenhoof, Lance Vance, like most Americans, had been brought up to believe in a personal God who could be appealed to for any trivial matter, and it was fairly likely that in acquiring his B.S. in Physical Education Lance had not been exposed to any ideas which might have sullied the naive purity of his childhood faith. The "professors" who had taught him Team Sports or Kinesiology had probably not required him to read much Nietzsche:

> Even the slightest trace of piety in us ought to make us feel that a God who cures a headcold at the right moment or tells us to get into a coach just as a downpour is about to start is so absurd a God he would have to be abolished even if he existed.
>
> (The Anti-Christ, 52)

Fr. Clovenhoof recalled seeing photos of adult football teams kneeling in prayer in their locker rooms, and wasn't there some outfit called the "Fellowship of Christian Athletes?" This union of the Cross and the Jockstrap was not, after all, so very odd in the U.S.A.

There certainly could be no doubt of Lance's sincerity in making his request. The whole way he had humbly entered the house, the deferential manner in which he sat on the couch with his huge scarred hands clasped between his knees, his beseeching tone of voice: all bespoke profound respect. Like a great many half-educated people, Lance Vance held all clergymen in high esteem. To him they were holy, elevated possessors of mystic powers. In fact, the coach on the couch was in the same state of intellectual development as some aborigine squatting by the door of a jungle hut, begging the witch doctor to come and help his wife escape a curse.

Fr. Clovenhoof realized all this in a flash, and he smiled. "Why, of course, coach. I'd be happy to pray with the team. What time? Six? Fine, I'll be there."

After the grateful athlete left, Fr. Clovenhoof retired to his study and mused on this development. He began to get an idea. The hockey team wanted help, did it? Maybe he could give them even more than they expected. He had for some time been intending to move from the purely intellectual realm of theology to the more practical. Why not start with a blessing for the hockey team? He went to the wall-sized bookcase and took down an old volume. He turned the pages thoughtfully until he came to, "Incantation for the Success of a Small Endeavour." He read it carefully. It didn't seem too risky.

The next evening Lance Vance and his twenty-three mercenaries appeared in chapel and Fr. Clovenhoof, feeling like a Landsknecht chaplain in the Schmalkaldic War, invoked the aid of Almighty God for His blessings in the coming battle. The little savages seemed heartened as they shuffled out.

An hour later, just before the game was starting, Fr. Clovenhoof was in the room across from his study, a small, bare room with curtains blocking the two windows. He was very excited as he stood in the center of the red chalk circle he had inscribed on the floor, a double circle with the words ADONAI, ELOHIM, TETRAGRAMMATON written between the lines and a large pentagram inside. The priest, wearing a hooded white robe and a wreath of vervain, lit the red candles at the pentagram's points and, holding a hazel wand in one hand and his grimoire in the other, recited the formula carefully and distinctly, ending with, "So be it, amen, amen, amen, fiat, fiat, fiat."

Nothing happened at all, except that one of the red candles went out—doubtless there was a draft under the door. Fr. Clovenhoof, who had not been sure what to expect, was simultaneously disappointed and relieved. He dressed warmly and walked to the arena. Arriving just at the end of the first quarter (or inning, or chukka, or whatever they're called), he saw Bruto Grubnecker score his second goal, and a glance at the score board showed SLA winning 4-1. The final score was 7-2, and Lance Vance, seeing the priest, came over, elated, and exclaimed, "Boy, padre, you sure can pray! This game went great."

"Did you expect to win it?" asked Fr. Clovenhoof.

"Oh, yeah, but not by this much. Our next game's on Tuesday. Would you come meet with the team again?"

"Yes, certainly," said the chaplain, wondering if his special ceremony had had anything to do with the victory. Time would tell.

XVIII. METROPOLIS

SLA was pretty much separate from the town of Vacheville. This separation was partly geographical, as the school was on the edge of town, but also because only a few day students attended SLA and life at the school kept everyone so busy that many faculty and students hardly ever left campus. The town did not like the school very much. Some Headmasters had discouraged interaction with the community, and the locals had a misconception that SLA was a bastion of wealth and privilege, an elitist enclave in a blue-collar milieu. Many citizens looked at the school the way the sans-culottes had viewed Versailles in 1789. That this was truly a misconception would have been clear to anyone who looked at SLA's balance sheet or SAT scores. The school, without being exactly on the brink of insolvency, had been forced to "borrow" over a million dollars from its own endowment, while the notion that SLA students were, as a group, pompous intellectuals, was an illusion fostered by the popular idea of what a "private school" is. In fact, there are independent schools of all kinds. There are some for geniuses and some for idiots. Some specialize in disciplinary problem cases and some in the musically gifted. Some have long waiting lists and some will take anyone, anytime. The image of a private school being a sort of Yuppie factory run by pipe-smoking gentlemen with leather patches on the sleeves of their tweed jackets is entirely erroneous (except for a few establishments in New England.)

Vacheville, the seat of Oat County, had a movie theater, a clothing store, a supermarket, a state prison, an insane asylum, a drugstore, a laundry, and an enormous number of bars and churches. There were Lutheran churches and Catholic churches and the Episcopal cathedral; there were Assemblies of God and Baptists (GARBC) and the generically-named Church of Christ, plus the United Church of Christ. There were Mormon churches and Congregational churches and Free Evangelical churches and the Jehovah's Witnesses and the United Methodists and the Nazarenes and the Seventh Day Adventists and the Charismatics. There was even a "Hispanic Evangelical Church," apparently for Catholic apostates. No variant of the basic theme was overlooked.

The architectural styles of these tabernacles was astonishing. Some were shacks and some were frame houses, some were stucco and some were concrete. One big Methodist church was graced by a huge dome of what appeared to be tin; it looked like a planetarium. Concealed in this dome was some sort of music system, and each day at noon a selection of hymn tunes would regale the passersby. This grotesque music box was put to shame, however, by the Catholic church about 500 yards away (across from the other Methodist structure, near the Episcopal cathedral.) It had apparently been built by a blind lunatic. To a basilica-like base with Romanesque windows and some Gothic features had been added a roof of half-cylindrical orange slates, as one might see on a Spanish hacienda. The triple-doored entrance, apparently modeled on that of Notre Dame de Paris, featured tympana bearing three bas-reliefs of devotional scenes: the Annunciation, Christ teaching the children, and Abraham about to sacrifice Isaac, this last one being a disconcerting contrast to the other two. Each scene was surmounted by a pointed arch, below which was carved in granite rectangles a weird medley of items: shamrocks, fleurs-de-lys, lillies, sunflowers, and little pot-bellied gnomes. Rising over fifty feet above this hodgepodge was a big bell tower built of brick, topped by four smaller columns and an octagonal cupola.

What in heaven this medley all meant would have taxed Thomas Aquinas to discover, and how this architectural crazy quilt had come to rise in a village in the middle of nowhere was a mystery.

But still....every noon there sounded from the tower the tolling of a single bell. It was, of course, electronically simulated. This was, after all, modern America, and there was no solitary eccentric living in the tower, devotedly tending his sanctified bells, like M. Carhaix in the novel by J.K. Huysmans. But those who had decent educations (and who could ignore the noises emanating from the Methodist juke box) paused just a bit when they heard it, for here was a direct link to the early Church, the tradition of a millennium transmitted to their daily lives. On Saturdays, when Mr. Jones walked downtown to do his shopping and to enjoy a gourmet meal at MacDonald's instead of Otto Auswurf's garbage, he heard that bell, and he always looked to see if all the cars would stop, and the shops close, and people fall to their knees in the street, and begin to pray. "Angelus Domini nuntiavit Mariae / Et concepit de Spiritu Sancto..." The Angelus was still there, by some miracle, despite ecumenism and Vatican II, proclaiming its historic truth amidst the profusion of heresies.

If Vacheville seemed to have 100 churches it must have had 200 bars and liquor stores. This was understandable. After all, winter in the area went from October through April, and while a visit to the First English Lutheran Church or the Full Gospel Sanctuary might provide solace for a Sunday, people needed some diversion for the other six days of the week.

The town had enough commerce to take care of the basic necessities of life. One could buy food at the Big-Little (the "Superette"), furniture at the "Ottoman Empire," and sundries at several small stores. Just the other day Mr. Jones had acquired not just a laundry bag, but what the label said was an "All-Purpose Laundry Bag." He had hoped to find inside a sheet explaining all the purposes to which his new laundry bag might be put, but there was none, so he just used it for his dirty clothes.

XIX. L'ÉTAT, C'EST LUI?

The Headmaster of SLA was the Rev. Dr. Elwood J. Dukesbury III, a man of forty-nine with a wife and two daughters. He lived in the Rectory, which was what the Headmaster's official residence was called. He had been at SLA for three years.

Headmasters of private schools are among the last people in the civilized world to exercise powers similar to those possessed by 18th-century European monarchs. This is not hyperbole. Most independent schools have no job security for their professional staff. There are no real contracts, no tenure, no appeals process, and certainly no unions. (The average groundskeeper, painter, or janitor at such a school does belong to a collective bargaining organization, which leads one to the conclusion that a good definition of an "educational professional" is a school worker who is too dumb to have a union.)

Headmasters also control where the faculty lives and how long they live there, what food they eat, what clothes they wear on duty, and, indeed, many aspects of their whole lives.

Absolute monarchs were responsible to God. A Headmaster answers to the Board of Trustees. The Board of a private school usually consists of about twenty people who serve without pay because they love the school, or are public-spirited, or were flattered to have been asked. Most are alumni. Most are wealthy, successful businessmen. They know nothing in particular about education, of course, and they therefore turn over to the Headmaster full authority to run the school as long as he doesn't lose money or annoy them in some way.

The SLA Board was at this time fairly bad. The chairman was a retired industrialist whose rubicund face and spherical body suggested that he was about to have a stroke, and he spent much of his time in hospitals. The Board members were mostly

76

people who remembered SLA as it had been many years before, and some still resented the loss of the ROTC program. Many had never spoken to a faculty member. The Episcopal bishop of the diocese, who was ex officio President of the Board, exercised great influence, especially in the selection and retention of the Headmaster, who was traditionally an Episcopal priest.

Now the ranks of this priesthood are quite motley, and from the collection of losers at his disposal Bishop Flamsteed had decided that E. John Dukesbury III was the best he could do for SLA. Dukesbury had taught at another school for a couple of years, his private life was respectable, and he had a Doctorate of Education, which seemed appropriate. (True, an Ed.D. degree has an actual value approximating that of a Certificate in Cosmetology from a third-rate vo-tech, except that a cosmetologist has to have some measurable skills, but the title "doctor" always goes down well with parents.) So the bishop used his influence to gain approval of his candidate, and E.J. Dukesbury was duly named Headmaster of St. Lawrence Academy.

It did not work out too badly. SLA had a history of fairly dreadful Headmasters, and at least Dr. Dukesbury wasn't an alcoholic or an embezzler, like a couple of his predecessors. He was merely stupid and dyslexic. This meant that his chief officers—the Director of Studies, the Dean, the Business Manager, etc.—had to work around him, and they were used to that. They edited his letters and gave him his ideas and generally controlled him well enough to prevent his doing serious harm.

Unfortunately there were times when Dr. Dukesbury had to be let loose on the public, and these could be disconcerting. His speeches were a mixture of jargon, malapropisms, spoonerisms, and just plain nonsense which produced pearls like, "I don't mean to be vague, but this is fuzzy," "We must refine our thinking internally," or "Most of these problems are explanatory."

Such gibberish actually produced less scorn or dismay than one might expect it to. So few people were willing to conclude that the emperor had no clothes that their reaction to something like, "We can solve these problems ourselves if we sort of get incestuous in a positive way," was a feeling that they had misheard the speaker, or that they were not intelligent enough to understand him. It didn't really matter, since no visitors were around, when the Headmaster buzzed the Academic Office and said to the two secretaries, Ms. Bondale and Ms. Safire, that he wanted to see Ms. Bonfire in his office. They were used to it; they looked at each other, smiled, and both went in.

Other faux pas were unnerving. When he misspelled the school's nickname (Bears) in a letter cheer at a pep rally, it was not good publicity. ("Gimmee a B!" "B!" "Gimmee an E!" "E!" Gimmee an R!" "R?" "Gimmee an A!" "...a..." "Gimmee an S!" "S!" "What have we got?" "Nothing, sir!")

Later that same evening, inspired to lead a snake dance around the football field, Dr. Dukesbury grabbed the nearest bystander and started off like crazy, only to discover that he had caught hold of a 73-year-old alumna, who plainly thought her last hour had come and that she was going to be dragged into the hereafter by a madman on Homecoming Weekend.

When meeting individuals Dr. Dukesbury could be effective for three or four minutes. His hypnotic eyes, bushy gray hair, firm chin, clerical garb, and pleasant, oleaginous voice made a good first impression, and the Admissions Director, Dean, or whoever was his keeper for the moment would get him moving before he revealed the yawning emptiness behind the façade. His wife, June, was a capable first lady and hostess, and his daughters were good students. SLA had seen worse. The trouble was, it had rarely seen better.

XX. THAT OLD BLACK MAGIC

November was a busy month for Asmodeus Clovenhoof. He was officiating at weekly chapels and by now he was making each one a unique experience. His love of ceremony fit well with the Student Vestry's desire for pomp, and with the introduction of hand bells and censers to the opening processions, chapel services were now noisier and smellier than ever. His sermons cleverly questioned such things as the divinity of Christ and the Resurrection, and suggested that the "temptation" episode of Matthew and Luke 4 was not so much a confrontation between opposites as a subtle description of how the two interdependent natures of divinity—represented by Jesus and Satan— between them controlled both the spiritual and physical worlds.

He was preparing his winter term course in Bible, a junior requirement. He looked forward to explaining the origins of monotheism by a study of Ishtar, Astarte, the Apis Bull, Dagon, and Baal, and to demonstrating that Jehovah was a combination of all of them.

His most enjoyable occupation, though, was his continuing relationship with the hockey team. His prayer sessions before home games were now a regular feature of the sports routine, and then came the special ceremony after it. He had used the same spell many times, and the team had won all of its games. One of the red candles always went out after each ceremony. Fr. Clovenhoof was elated at this apparent success of his first essays into practical thaumaturgy.

Then came a new development. The team was going away for a weekend tourney against a club in Winnipeg, a very strong opponent. Lance Vance confided that he doubted SLA would win, "especially since you won't be there to pray with us," he said with a laugh.

Fr. Clovenhoof believed that this was a fine time to test his powers. On Friday night he did nothing, then called Lance Vance. The team had lost, 4-1, and two players had been slightly injured. "We're going to get creamed tomorrow," lamented the coach.

"Don't worry," said the priest. "Tell the boys I'll be praying for them."

He had no duty on Saturday, so he could spend all day preparing for his experiment. He had decided to try a stronger conjuration, and there was much to be done. He had to inscribe certain names of power on parchment with a silver pen using special ink, prepare a mixture of assafoetida and pitch for his copper braziers, and procure a live chicken.

That night, at the hour when the game was starting, he stood in the center of his pentagram and set to work, reciting the words from the Grimoire of Honorious, burning the foul incense, and causing the chicken to be no longer alive.

This time Asmodeus Clovenhoof did not have to wonder if he had accomplished anything, because as he reached the words, "Conjuro te, spiritus magnus, in nomine Astaroth," and burned a sprig of nightshade, two red spots appeared, hovering outside the circle in the dark room , and a voice sounded inside the priest's head, "What wilt thou, O master?"

He almost fainted with excitement. "Master!" He spoke his request and read the dismissal spell. All the candles went out and the red spots vanished.

The chaplain felt exhausted as he left the chamber. At 11:00 his phone rang. It was Coach Vance. SLA had crushed the enemy, 7-2. Bruto Grubnecker had done the hat trick. It was, said Lance, "a miracle."

"Well, you might say that," chuckled Fr. Clovenhoof. "Remember, I was praying for you."

This wonderful success so delighted him that he at once began even deeper studies in his collection of theurgic texts and mystical arcana. He wrote to a trusted friend, a fellow-student at the seminary who now held a cure of souls in Oregon while casting horoscopes in his spare time, to ask that he make him a wand of ash as soon as possible. He began to plan more potent conjurations.

XXI. THE UNEXAMINED LIFE IS NOT WORTH LIVING

Fall Term final exams were approaching, a time of stress and anxiety for many students. Those who had worked during the previous ten weeks were not upset, since they would do well, but the lazy and the stupid trembled in terror. The final, worth about one-third of the term grade, would finish them off.

Mr. Jones had brought his course to 1793. This was an awkward spot to stop, four years into the French Revolution, but that could not be helped. Every year the school fiddled with the calendar, so it was quite impossible to know in advance where he would be when the term ended. Some years classes began around August 22, some years a week later; sometimes the term ran until Thanksgiving, with that week off for fall break, and other times finals came in the first or second week in November (which meant bringing everyone back a week before Thanksgiving, then trying to send them away again when that holiday arrived, then having three weeks of classes until Christmas break began.) Calendar decisions were controlled by arcane forces, none of which were connected with academics. For example, the date set by the State High School League for the opening of basketball practice was usually in mid-November, so if the school was then closed the hoopsters would lose invaluable practice time. With the calendar built largely around the demands of athletics, and the athletic calendar designed by and for public schools, every year SLA did a dance trying to align the realities of a boarding school with the schedules of public schools. SLA had not had the same calendar two years in a row in living memory.

Some of the more eccentric teachers at SLA occasionally wished that sports were not so important and at least one dreamer spoke wistfully of a prep school which had no interscholastic sports at all. However, no one was so silly as actually to propose such a thing. After all, SLA was a preparatory school, and all its graduates would be going to American colleges and universities. There, athletics ruled the roost, and many of the "students" were recruited for their athletic skills, and were recipients of, to use a wonderful oxymoron, "athletic scholarships." These "institutions of higher learning" served as farm programs and training camps for professional football, basketball, and hockey, with all the innumerable abuses and massive corruption which go with the sports business. The cult of athletics is so entrenched in American life that nothing short of the outright abolition of those college sports which can lead to professional careers would cure the disease. And where would we be without a Rose Bowl or a Final Four? Why, people would go mad with boredom and fling themselves from bridges.

One often hears that American higher education is the best in the world. This is rubbish. American colleges and universities are, to be sure, the best <u>trade schools</u> in the world. They turn out well-trained workmen of various kinds—computer experts, mechanical engineers, hotel managers, pharmacists, and the like—so why should they not turn out professional athletes, too? The idea that a <u>university education</u> is something which by its very nature is limited to a tiny percentage of the population, and that the vast majority of the featherless bipeds who inhabit the earth could no more complete a real education than they could fly, because they are not intelligent enough, and that the only real <u>education</u> is in the liberal arts, everything else being job-training (which is of course a good and praiseworthy and beneficial and necessary thing, but it is not <u>education</u>) is hardly an idea which will gain acceptance in our insanely egalitarian age. So what if the average graduate from the average U.S. college would hardly be considered worthy of sweeping the floor at Oxford or the Sorbonne? So what if we have a nation whose "educated" adults still listen to rock music, watch hours of television sports and sitcoms, and haven't read <u>War and Peace</u>? You don't want to be considered an "elitist," do you? So why should it be thought that a university education should make you different from anyone else, or even different than you were before you started it, except in the acquisition of some mechanical skills enabling you to earn money?

In the very early days of college football, a team asked the university president if it could miss a day of classes to go away and play another institution. The president replied, "I refuse to allow twenty men to travel a hundred miles in order to agitate a bag of wind." What has gone wrong since that happy day? How did the foul hand of professional athletics ever fasten its evil, corrupting grip around the neck of American education?

Probably it is due to innate, and possibly ineradicable, defects in the American character. After all, nothing like it exists elsewhere. Europe does not go gaga over some annual Cambridge- Heidelberg soccer match.

Well, at any rate, final examinations at SLA often came at places inconvenient for the academic courses, but they had to make the best of it. In the case of Mr. Jones's MEH course, breaking off in 1793 at least gave him the fun of writing on each end-of-term comment, "We start the next term with the Reign of Terror," a remark which parents could interpret in various ways.

To prepare students for the final, Mr. Jones gave them two essay questions a week in advance, one of which would actually appear on the test. He gave them a review sheet containing the names of every person, every date, every term and event, for which they were responsible. He spent two days reviewing in class, and, in addition to the regular, daily extra help, he was available from 6:30 to 8:00 on the Sunday night before the Monday-morning test—a test which actually covered, not the whole term, but only the last two weeks of it, the French material.

Nonetheless, many of his students were terrified, panic-stricken, especially the new students, those who were in their first year at SLA. They would actually have to <u>know</u> <u>things</u> for this test, things like what was the Tennis Court Oath and the

84

Brunswick Manifesto and why the Revolution appeared doomed by the spring of 1793. And they would have to write an <u>essay</u>, something three or even four pages long, in a blue book. Nothing in their public-school careers had prepared them for this frightful ordeal, this awesome challenge. No wonder the MEH course had so fearsome a reputation as a breaker of men, a destroyer of brains, an academic Juggernaut crushing students beneath its pitiless wheels.

Over half of the fifty-two students in the course did sensible things. They carefully reviewed their notes and the readings, they drew up essay outlines and brought them in for Mr. Jones to look over, and they studied the review sheet.

The other students did senseless things. Several, despairing of being able to construct their own essays, paid money to others to write them for them, and they memorized these ghostwritten essays without any idea of what they meant. Others, gamblers at heart, carefully prepared one essay but not the other, figuring they had a fifty-fifty chance of getting the one they wanted. A few decided to cheat outright. One boy procured two blue books and wrote one essay in each, intending to smuggle them in and hand in the appropriate one. Several prepared crib sheets to be cleverly concealed upon their persons. A couple wrote information on their hands (a "date palm.") Two, who happened to be in ESSH, where the test would be held next morning, wrote material on the desk tops, intending to sit there for the test.

Most of these efforts were in vain. Mr. Jones was a thorough man. The blue books he handed out for the test had the date stamped on them in red, so the student with the pre-written essays did not dare to turn in his obviously supposititious ones. The information written on the desk tops mysteriously disappeared by morning, because Mr. Jones had gone up to the study hall at 10:15 PM with a rag and a bottle of cleaner and scoured all 115 desks. No one was allowed to bring any books or papers into the room.

On the test day Mr. Jones and his colleague Ms. Green, the World Cultures teacher, whose freshmen were being tested in the same room, spent all two hours on their feet, in ceaseless vigilance of the laboring students. (SLA did not subscribe to any "honor system" in giving tests. Not even a pretense was made of trusting anybody. On the contrary, the official, admirably realistic doctrine was that virtually anyone who thought he could get away with cheating would cheat.)

About half an hour into the exam, a boy got up to get a drink of water. Mr. Jones walked to the student's desk, near the back of the room, to turn over his test sheet so the girl sitting behind couldn't see any answers. And lo!, as he flipped it over a piece of paper about three inches square fell out and landed on the floor. Mr. Jones picked it up and glanced at it. "Girondists = Liberals," he read. "Jacobins = Radicals. 1789 - Estates-General meets, becomes Nat'l Assy." Lots of other interesting information was crammed close together. Mr. Jones grinned, and, seeing that the student, still drinking at the fountain in the front of the room, had no idea what had happened, he put the slip of paper in his pocket and strolled away.

When the boy returned to his desk Mr. Jones enjoyed covertly watching him from across the room as he began to look for his crib sheet, first casually, then with increasing agitation, flipping through the pages of his blue book, feeling under his desk. Mr. Jones's <u>Schadenfreude</u> was intensified by his knowledge that the student, Paul Virek, was already on probation after an unopened can of beer had been found in his room in September. He was in peril, and now he was becoming terrified as the thin strands holding aloft the sword of Damocles fast unravelled.

After gloating for a couple of minutes, Mr. Jones sauntered over to Virek's desk. He smiled evilly and held up the cheat sheet. "Looking for something, Paul?" he whispered. Then he swiftly picked up the test sheet and the blue book and said, "OK, come with me." He signalled to Ms. Green that he would be gone for a minute or two and he escorted Paul to the office of the Director of Studies.

"Hi, George. Got a little unpleasant business for you, I'm afraid," he said, putting the test materials and the crib sheet on the desk.

George Fong glanced at the totally disconsolate student standing behind Mr. Jones and said, "Oh, dear, Paul, I guess you don't really want to be here, do you? Sit down."

Mr. Jones returned to the big test room happy in the knowledge that he would now have just fifty-one MEH finals to grade, instead of fifty-two.

(About two hours later, after the Headmaster had concurred with Mr. Fong's recommendation to dismiss, Paul Virek was taken to the airport and put on a plane to his home in Iowa. The housemasters boxed and mailed his belongings over the next weeks. Nobody at SLA ever saw him again.)

Two hours were allowed for each final exam, but few students took that long, nor did their teachers expect them to. Seventy-five to ninety minutes were enough for most English and History tests (which require more writing than Science or Math). But finals do need more than, say, forty minutes to do decently, and there was a rule that no one could leave until the first hour was up. It was interesting to see which students finished early, closed their blue books, and even put their heads down. The exam had started at 9:00. At 10:00 Mr. Jones announced jovially, "Those who are finished with my test may now leave, but please save me some time by putting a large F on the front of your blue book." About eight students slunk out anyway. Among them were some who had bought outlines and complete essays from geniuses and had spent a little while reproducing their memorized material without understanding it. These essays were often funny. It was not uncommon for a student to get halfway through one and for his mind to then go off the rails. For example, many European rulers are named Charles. On one occasion Mr. Jones was reading an essay dealing with the English Civil War when King Charles I suddenly stopped being a Stuart, became a Hapsburg, and by his death brought about the War of the Spanish Succession. The student writing the essay had combined England in the 1640's with Spain sixty years later. On another occasion one poor wretch, having memorized "Essay A" and "Essay B", as they were designated on the sheet given out a week before the test, was totally disconcerted when, on the actual examination, the chosen essay question was printed without an "A" or a "B" before it. The flummoxed lummox couldn't recall which of his memorized essays went with which question! He took a guess and wrote the wrong one. Then there was the case of the boy who had learned an answer to "Essay A," received what he knew was "Essay B," realized he did not know enough to write anything worthwhile, and submitted his test with the written comment, "Mr. Jones—Sorry, I guess I'm not a good gambler." (Mr. Jones, sympathetic as ever, had written, "I guess you're not," just below the big red zero he gave him for his essay.)

Occasionally there would be a howler. One essay, on life in France before the Revolution, had begun, "I am a poor peasant. Each morning I get up and cook my breakfast on my wooden stove." After Mr. Jones had finished convulsing over this gem, he had written on the test, "No wonder the peasants were so poor: they had to keep buying new stoves. 'Hey, Pierre, come queek, ze stove she is on fire again.' I think you mean a <u>wood</u> stove." Nor could Mr. Jones easily forget the reference, in an essay on the aftermath of Italian unification, to the doctrine, defined by Vatican I, of "Papal Inflammability." (Considering the personality of Pope Pius IX, and his state of mind after the Papacy lost all of its territory by 1871, "inflammability" was actually quite a perceptive description.) Also memorable were the girl who described the Russian nihilist organization, the People's Will, as "the group of terrorists that tried (and succeeded) many times in killing Tsar Alexander II", and the phonetic speller who called France's most famous queen "Mary-Ann Twanette."

Once there had been a student who just didn't care—a bright but very lazy boy contemptuous of school. On his winter term final, the topic of which had been the career of Camillo Cavour, the brilliant diplomat who played so major a role in the Risorgimento, he had written the following "essay:"

> Cavour's gonna go down in history
> Just 'cause he unified Italy.
> Who cares about a country that's got no loot?
> Who cares about a country that's shaped like a boot?

Mr. Jones had read this little poem at the end-of-term faculty meeting, and everyone had gotten a lot of chuckles over the cheeky insouciance of the student who had submitted it. When the teachers had finished chuckling they voted to inform the boy, who was by then home on vacation, that his things would be mailed to him, and that he need not return for the spring term.

Almost all of the students were gone by 10:40, but, as always, a few remained. A couple of these were extraordinarily good scholars who had a lot to say, all of which would be relevant. What they wrote would be a pleasure to read and would be especially welcome to Mr. Jones, because it would show him that he was actually teaching something to somebody. (He occasionally doubted it, you see. Since the school had lowered its already modest admission standards in order to recruit champion athletes, Mr. Jones was teaching a couple of sections in which he sometimes had the eerie feeling that he was talking to himself. On one occasion he had barely been able to resist leaving his classroom and going outside to lecture to the birds, like Francis of Assisi. It was difficult to keep one's mind on the intricacies of presenting the Diplomatic Revolution of 1756 to sophomores, in a way they could understand it, when four or five little savages were ignoring you completely and drawing crossed sticks surrounded by the words "SLA Hockey" on their desks.)

A few of the late-stayers were weak students who really wanted to do their best, and were carefully checking their matching and multiple-choice sections, re-reading their essays, and worrying about their chronologies. And then there were the usual neurotics, sitting there amidst a jumble of pencils, erasers, and jars of Liquid Paper, intent on turning in exams with no smudges, cross-outs, or mechanical errors.

By 11:10 Mr. Jones had cajoled everyone into finishing, for he hated to take tests away forcibly, and was on his way home for five enjoyable days of reading exams and writing comments, his conscientious labors made no easier by the knowledge that most students did about the same on their finals as they had done all term and that the final would therefore make no real difference in their grade. Occasionally a B student would write a D final or a D student would earn a C+ for the term, but this was rare. (Every year, as finals approached, some student who was failing the course would ask Mr. Jones, "What will happen if I get an A on the final?" The teacher's standard answer was, "I'll faint dead away.")

After grading finals no teachers felt like writing full comments, but fortunately most of these could be done mechanically, as has been explained. Comments on some students could be difficult because one could not always say what one really wanted to. Once an anonymous teacher had typed up and posted in the faculty lounge a "comment I'd like to write," using a fictional student name:

> I assume the reason why this moron is here is that his parents took a wrong turn on the way to the State Hospital. Orville has spent his time scribbling obscenities on his desk, unnerving me with his lobotomized stare, and drooling in his lap. While he might someday, by dint of extensive training and laborious study, become a passable village idiot, his only current utility is as an example of why abortion is sometimes a good idea. I suggest that his parents consider euthanasia.

There weren't more than four or five students at SLA to whom this might have applied.

XXII. FURTHER DEVELOPMENTS

"This is just marvellous work, Mario. You've tripled the Annual Giving pledges, you've gotten over 3.4 million in deferred gifts, and this legacy from Arthur Hobart is so welcome—over 1.4 million. We may actually be able to implement some of our architects' plans." The Headmaster paused and picked up a newspaper clipping from among the papers spread on his desk. "Mr. Hobart's death was quite tragic, though. Why would a man of his years and wealth be wandering along the railroad tracks after midnight? What a terrible accident. They couldn't even find his head!"

"Yes, sir, but you know he was unstable. Look at that Rosicrucian fad he was into before our consultants, uh, reasoned him out of it." The burly Development Director was sitting in front of the Headmaster's baroque desk, uncomfortably stuffed into one of the fragile antique chairs.

"True, true. Yes, that Chicago firm has done wonders for us. You say their personal visits have been 100% successful?"

"Sure have, boss. Those guys are really persuasive."

"Well, it's just wonderful, Mario. You keep up the wood gurk, I mean the good work. You're really solving our deficit problems."

Mr. Pestalozzi left and went happily back to his department. When he got there, Mary Coster smiled and said, "Oh, Mario, there's a Mr. Ammazarlo here to see you. And you know what? We just received a letter from the actor, Mark Brodan, who's never given us one cent in the thirty-seven years since he graduated. He sent a check for $30,000 and said he'll be sending more as soon as he's out of the hospital. He had a narrow escape from a hit-and-run driver."

"That's great, Mary," said her boss, going into his private office and closing the door.

The man who rose to greet him was tall and thin, about fifty, with a nose that was not aligned with the rest of his face.

"How are ya, Mad Dog?" he asked with a smile as they shook hands.

"Great, Roberto—but remember, I asked you never to use my nickname here. I won't be calling you Knuckles any more."

"Oh, yeah, sorry," said Mr. Ammazarlo as they sat down. "Old habits die hard. Look, this operation's goin' great so far. Easiest money we ever made. But the reason I came is that the Capo di Tutti Capi is thinkin' that ten per cent is a little small for our cut."

"Don Benito thinks that?" asked Mario. "But hell, theoretically we're paying you guys just $8,000 a month. It's tricky to deduct the rest when checks come in or a will is probated."

"Yeah, the Don knows. So what we're going to do is have the Family's lawyers take over from that local firm of ambulance-chasers you got workin' for ya. Once Feinberg, Axelrod, and Weintraub are handling this stuff, these financial arrangements will be no problem."

Mario thought for a moment. "I ought to be able to arrange that," he said. "How much more does the Don want?"

"Just three per cent," said Roberto. "He's reasonable. And he's gonna expand your operation by adding another soldier. There's a lot of these alumnis to call on." He took a list from his violin case. "Just on the West Coast alone there's seventy-two more people to see."

"Mary only gave you the fat cats, right? I don't want to waste time on some sciagurato that's got no dough."

"Oh, yeah, natch. Your guys don't interview anybody who can't kick in at least $25,000 a year. After all, we are not Communists."

"While you're here, Roberto, there's a new thing I want to talk to you about. We've got a real stone in our shoe." He buzzed for John Fordiss, and said, "John, do you have the file on Mr. Orgule handy?"

"Yes, sure, Mario." He brought it in. "Gee," he said as he handed him the file, "do you really think that Mr. Orgule will support the school? He told us years ago to take him off our mailing list."

"Well, Mr. Ammazarlo here is coordinating our efforts, and he'll see to it that our representatives give Mr. Orgule a new kind of presentation, which I think will help him see the light."

John beamed at Mr. Ammazarlo. "Gosh, you guys have done such good work for us, sir. I sure hope you can help here."

"Thanks, kid. I just bet we'll get this guy in a real generous mood. In fact, when we get done with our presentation, he'll probably wish he had even more money he could give us."

Roberto and Mario laughed heartily as the young assistant left. Mario opened the folder.

"Charles Orgule never graduated. He was here three years, a B student, but three weeks before commencement he was caught with a girl in his room. They were both expelled. He got a diploma from some public school in Iowa, served in Korea, and went to college under the G.I. Bill. Graduated Iowa State in 1958 with a major in electrical engineering. Then he went to California where he and a friend started a computer company. Got in on the ground floor. In 1977 IBM bought them out for $455 million. He has three kids, none of whom he sent to SLA. He hangs up on the phonathon. He doesn't answer letters. Apparently he's still sore about being tossed out just before graduation after being here three years. I think it's about time he shared the wealth."

"Definitely," agreed Roberto, taking the file. "I'll pass this along to the troops. But this guy is probably gonna need lots of persuading. I'll send the whole team." He rose to leave. "Oh, by the way, that Mrs. Faraway, the bubble gum heiress who pledged $1.6 million? You can plan on that will being probated real soon. In fact, just as soon as the old girl takes the special nitroglycerin capsule that Alfredo put in her pill case while he was visiting her."

"Thanks, Roberto," said Mario, walking his colleague to the door. "And good luck with Charlie Orgule."

XXIII. NEW TERM, OLD HABITS

At 11:45 on the first Monday of Winter Term the fourth period and the assembly were over and the school trooped into the refectory for lunch. It was immediately apparent that Otto Auswurf's culinary skills had not improved over the vacation. To welcome everyone back the kitchen was serving the "sandwich spread special." This consisted of giving each table a bowl of yellow paste with the courtesy title of "egg salad," and a bowl of some hideous greenish-pink substance whimsically called "ham salad." The latter was so noxious that hardly anyone ever tried it. These delicacies were served with pita bread, a thick, leathery substance slit to make a tiny wallet, which could be filled with the spreads. It tasted like moldy cardboard. There was also a plate of sliced tomatoes so garishly red that one could almost see the chemical dye oozing out of them, and some radishes sour enough to spoil your whole day. About forty small salads were at the salad bar; when they were gone, no more appeared. For beverages one could have (a) milk or (b) water. Coffee at lunch had been abolished two years before, officially for reasons of health but really to save a little money. Kool-Aid had been discontinued at the same time because some of the younger students would gulp down four or five glasses and be on a hyperactive sugar high all afternoon.

Mr. Jones, sitting at his accustomed table with a new group of students—they were rotated randomly every two weeks— made a few old jokes about the cuisine, filled out the attendance slip, forced down some "egg salad," took a hearty swing of milk, and sprang to his feet, choking and knocking over his chair. He rushed over to a food cart and voided his mouthful of milk into its refuse bin. It was rancid. The bottom half-inch of his milk carton was curdled muck. Nor had he been uniquely unfortunate: all over the room people were gasping for air as they threw away the expired containers.

Mr. Jones sat down and rinsed his mouth with water. "Good lord," he said, "this is too much. These meals are impossible."

"They sure are," agreed Tom Peterson, the senior at the other end of the table. (Each table was assigned one senior, who sat at the opposite end and acted as table head if the teacher was absent. If more than one senior was assigned, the one who had been at the school longest—the senior senior—had the privilege.) "Geez, I just got back from a week of home cooking, and now this."

"Mr. Auswurf ought to be fired," put in a freshman girl, who had refused to eat anything.

Then came dessert. The student waiters brought out plates of things called "seven layer bars." Four of the layers were of half-cooked batter, two were of pure sugar, and one was an unidentifiable turquoise paste which probably glowed in the dark. A couple of students nibbled at them.

The student proctor who had collected the absence slips walked up the stairs to High Table, the dais against the wall on one side of the big room where the Headmaster, his wife, and a few students (rotated like the others) ate on a white tablecloth with crystal glassware and sterling silver utensils. (The food was the same, though, except that Dr. Dukesbury could have coffee.) The proctor picked up the old brass bugle and blew it loudly—this was a tradition left over from the military days— and, when silence reigned, made the daily announcements from slips of paper handed him by various faculty members and activity heads. Girls' basketball had early practice, the Dramatics Society would meet at 6:30. When the proctor said, "Any further announcements?" a voice called out, "Yeah. We want some decent food!"

A storm of applause swept the hall and many looked towards the big double door of the kitchen to see of Otto Auswurf would appear, but he did not. The proctor dismissed the seniors—leaving the dining hall first was one of their minor privileges—and then the underformers.

There were fifteen minutes before the fifth-period class began. Mr. Jones, after mentally checking to see if there was anything he could get done in that time, and finding, to his surprise, that there was not, wandered out into the main hallway, idly turning down the Senior Corridor (so-called because of the only students who traditionally could enter it.) This long corridor was the main entrance to Laud Hall, and was designed to impress visitors. The floor was covered by a rich red carpet and set with big, elaborately-carved oaken tables and four huge chairs dating from the nineteenth century. (At commencement one of these thrones was taken to the chapel for the use of the Bishop when he presided at the closing service.) There was a charmingly-decorated sitting room on one end, and a spacious "powder room" next to it. The Headmaster's office and the Admissions Department were also located there. The walls were of dark walnut to a height of about five feet, then yellow paper to the ceiling. Along these walls hung portraits of the great men of the school: the donors, founders, and distinguished Headmasters. These paintings were all half-figures, and as Mr. Jones walked by them he wondered, not for the first time, if the people they depicted had really looked like that. They almost all had beetling brows, full beards, and black coats, coats which faded into the black of the paintings' backgrounds and made Senior Corridor appear to be decorated by disembodied heads floating about seven feet up. None of these people looked as though they had ever laughed or cried.

No one had labelled the pictures. There were spaces for labels at the bottoms of the frames, but they were empty. Who were they?   Did they ever really exist at all?   Mr. Jones wondered if there was a private school supply house somewhere, perhaps in England, where one could buy portraits of generic patriarchs and save whole decades of time simply by hanging a number of intimidating "old" paintings around your school, creating a sort of instant tradition to awe the public.

Mr. Jones continued his peripatetic musings as he left Laud Hall, turned left, and climbed the steps to the gymnasium/library wing. As he came to the doors he saw on the wall the old bronze plaque engraved with the name of a long-forgotten alumnus, the date 1908, and the words,

> The main thing in life is to do well something that is worth doing.
> Care not for show: life is too short and too sacred for make-believe.

Mr. Jones paused, as he always did whenever he passed this memorial, because he thought that it was one of the best things at the school. He often wondered what influence the fine words had had on the thousands of people who passed it yearly. Had this alumnus said it, or had he found it somewhere? Whatever the case, Mr. Jones was glad the plaque was there (although it was so small, and blended so well with the dark-red wall it was on, that it was easy to miss it.)

Then he passed through the doors and turned down the corridor outside the gymnasium. Here his attention was arrested by another plaque, of very recent vintage. It was actually a huge sign, seven feet wide and about nine high, bolted to the wall overhead and bearing words in bold red letters on a gray background. One could not help but see it. It bore a long quotation by a man whom someone thought could serve as a moral guide for the young people at SLA. Who was this inspiring guide? Shakespeare? Churchill? Ghandi? Well, no... The philosopher Plato? No... Mr. Jones read the flaming words:

> Winning is not a sometime thing. You don't win once in awhile. You don't do things right once in awhile. You do them right all the time.
> Winning is a habit. So is losing. There is no room for second place... . It is and always has been an American zeal to be first in anything we do, and to win, and to win, and to win.

I firmly believe that any person's finest hour, their greatest fulfillment to all that is held dear, is the moment when one has worked one's heart out in a good cause and lies exhausted on the field of battle victorious.

Thus spoke the philosopher Lombardi. And how right it was to give such ringing words so prominent a place, thought Mr. Jones. True, the sign was semi-literate: "zeal" misused, "awhile" should have been two words, "their" did not agree with "person's," "fulfillment to" was wrong, and the first four sentences were patently false, but why be pedantic? What could better summarize the new spirit which animated St. Lawrence Academy since the advent of the hockey program? (It was, of course, Lance Vance who had caused the sign to be erected.) The great Vince Lombardi on winning all the time: so much more appropriate, in every way, than some old fossil prating about truth, or honor, or justice, or, or even knowledge, at a school....

Mr. Jones's musings were interrupted by the five-minute bell. He went to a water fountain to try to wash out the lingering taste of sour milk, and then began climbing the stairs to his classroom on the third floor. In doing this he passed by an office, and heard a voice call his name. He went in and saw Mike Flan, the newly-hired Director of Student Services (i.e., the school shrink.)

"I know you've got a class, John, but I wanted to touch bases with you about Aaron White. I've been getting copies of flunk slips from most of his teachers and I know he's doing poorly in everything. I wanted your input as to what the trouble is. Do you think this boy has Tourette's syndrome, or discalculia, or narcolepsy? Maybe it's an endocrine imbalance, or an eating disorder? Do you think Aaron is L.D., or A.D.H.D., or maybe even E.B.D?"

Mr. Jones glanced at the wall clock and saw he had only a minute to get to class. Fortunately, he had very definite views on Aaron White. "No," he said. "I think he's just S.T.U.P.I.D."

The young councilor blinked. "Oh? Now that's a condition I'm not familiar with. It must be new to the literature."

Mr. Jones headed for the door, saying as he left, "Actually, Mike, it's a very old one. I believe that Socrates often encountered it in Athens."

Mr. Jones entered his class just as the bell rang, walked to the podium, counted the students, noted those absent, and immediately launched into the day's lesson. First he reviewed the final exam, and, since the fall term's end had cut the Revolution in half, he also reviewed the period 1789-1793.

France was on the brink of collapse. The First Coalition— all of Europe except Russia—was attacking on all fronts. Toulon had fallen, betrayed to the English. General Dumouriez had deserted to the enemy. Soldiers and supplies were scarce. The Austrians and the Prussians had recovered Belgium and the Rhineland. The Girondists were revolting in many major cities. Now was the time for the Jacobins to demonstrate how to run a revolution. Danton, St. Just, Robespierre, and their friends, would now take charge. La patrie en danger! Tout le monde a la bataille! How would they save France? Stay tuned to this lectern...and read pp. 160 to 162 for tomorrow, there might be a reading quiz.

The class ended, the fourth and final Modern Europe section of the day. Mr. Jones had a free period now, then his Twentieth Century Europe section to close the afternoon. He went to his mailbox—both personal and professional mail came to the school, of course—and walked the hundred yards to his shack. As he walked along it occurred to him that the Jacobins believed in winning all the time, and that the only way they could have saved the revolution was to win, and to win, and to win. Perhaps he could make his course more "relevant," as history teachers were always being urged to do, by telling his students that

Maximilien Robespierre was the Vince Lombardi of the Eighteenth Century?

In addition to the educational ads, textbook blurbs, seminar announcements, and other material related to teaching and professional development, all of which he automatically threw out without reading, he saw that he had received the <u>Chronicle of Higher Education</u>, the semi-official weekly newspaper of the college world.   Mr. Jones subscribed to this journal partly because he wanted to keep some contact with Higher Education even though he himself was in Lower Education and also because he liked to read the want ads. He still hoped to teach at a college. Or at least he thought he hoped to. Recently he was not so sure. The apparent emphasis on "political correctness" worried him, since he himself was politically somewhere to the right of Louis XIV. He was also irritated by the "EOE/AA" (Equal Opportunity Employer / Affirmative Action) rubric which one saw at the end of almost every advertisement. Mr. Jones was all for EOE, but it seemed to him that AA was its opposite. How like the liberals, he thought, to come up with an oxymoron and call it a solution to a problem.

Whenever he expressed interest in a job in Higher Education, he received things through the mail which amazed him. A form would arrive which asked him to fill in his "race," and the "races" were listed: White (not Hispanic), Hispanic, Black, Oriental, American Indian/Alaskan, Pacific Islander. The USA had become the most race-conscious society since Germany in the 1930's. Didn't anthropology recognize only three races? Would not someone from Madrid consider himself "white?" But then, under the US racial code, people from Spain were not Hispanic, were they? How did you prove your race? What made you an official Black? And these forms, these cards, all said on them that the information was being gathered "for statistical purposes only" and would have "no effect on the application." This encouraging news was usually printed right above the line where you were supposed to fill in your name.

On one occasion Mr. Jones had felt so indignant that he wrote on the form, "I hope you manage to find the black woman with a Spanish surname you're so obviously looking for." He had not heard again from that school.

Lately there had been even more grotesque developments in this area. Mr. Jones had received from one college a form requesting a list of the candidate's "impairments," and a list of possible responses was helpfully included:

TYPE OF IMPAIRMENTS ACCORDING TO THE FOLLOWING DEFINITIONS:

Physical: Amputee; Polio; Paralysis; Diabetic; Cardio-vascular; Paraplegia; Quadraplegia (sic); Epilepsy; Tuberculosis; Arthritis/Rheumatism; Visual; Hearing; Speech

Mental: Emotionally Disturbed; Learning Disability; Mental Retardation

Other Related: Alcoholism; Drug Abuse/Addiction

Mr. Jones had read this thing at the end of a duty day, i.e., at 10:30 PM. He had become momentarily confused. Did this school mean to imply that an impairment was a desirable thing for its professors to have? Had an impairment quota been introduced? Were the liberals at ———— University concerned because too few of their colleagues were epileptics? Was there a National Association for the Advancement of Drug Addicts which was angry because of the paucity of its members on university faculties? Had the ACLU stepped in? Did the most desirable candidate have, perhaps, one impairment from each category? Was the school really hoping to find a female tubercular mentally retarded alcoholic from the Pacific Islands?

In his confused state, Mr. Jones had begun to regret that he did not qualify. He _did_ smoke. Would that help? Could that be

102

an "addiction?" Could he, perhaps, enhance his professional qualifications for Higher Education by buying a wheelchair and pretending to need it?

This situation seemed insane, but it was not entirely new. Nothing is. Athens had reached a point, around 485 B.C., where the members of the Boulé, the executive council, were chosen by lot instead of elected. That was true democracy: no discrimination because of ability. Everyone was qualified. Athens had collapsed in 404.

Mr. Jones sometimes thought he would be very unhappy teaching college. Colleges seemed to be dominated by modern liberalism, and modern liberalism seemed to be a sort of brain disease.

The disease was also contagious: it was being caught by independent schools. Mr. Jones recalled an evening not long before, when he returned from a faculty meeting with a rectangular green booklet which had so impressed the Headmaster that he had issued copies to all the teachers. It had been produced by the regional affiliate of the NAIS (National Association of Independent Schools) to which SLA belonged. This affiliate, called, rather Biblically, ESAU (Elementary and Secondary Academic Union) consisted of...well, actually, Mr. Jones didn't know much about it, since its main purpose seemed to be arranging the evaluation visits for member schools which, like plagues of locusts, occurred every seven years, and were almost as annoying. When it was not evaluating its 200+ schools, ESAU confected books and pamphlets on education for the edification of teachers. This green thing was a fair example.

Mr. Jones usually did not read such things, because he was a reactionary, but, thinking that he should at least sample the latest in pedagogical ideas, he had decided to read this one, which was alliteratively entitled, "Preparing for Probable and Preferable Futures."

The booklet certainly produced an effect on Mr. Jones. The effect was similar to that promised by the ghost of Hamlet's father, should he describe Hell: it made his "knotted and combined locks to part, and each particular hair to stand on end."

It was not the first few pages which upset Mr. Jones. He was not disturbed that the booklet began by assuming that independent education needed, as a matter of course, "systemic, holistic, paradigm-shifting change," and that only a minority of dullards would confine themselves to "work on a smaller scale, introducing adjustments slowly," because he knew that any educational association worth its salt could never be satisfied with the status quo. He was not upset by the list of "Striking Statistics, with implications for education, schools, teachers," thirty-four items including "Persons living alone grew from 8% to 25% of U.S. households in the last fifty years," "Five years is suggested by the literature for bringing about major school-wide change," and "the average American burns 2 1/2 times more energy than the Japanese" (he supposed this should have been "a Japanese" rather than all of them) because he couldn't see any implications in all of this for teaching European history to sophomores. He was only a little bit upset by the examples of how to solve two of the "ten vital questions"—diversity and conflict resolution—because the booklet's prose was so weird that he couldn't take them very seriously:

> How are the following kinds of conflicts currently identified: trustee-head, administration-faculty, faculty-faculty, parent-faculty, student-faculty, student-student, parent-child, staff-faculty, student-staff?

> What ethnic, gender, class, nationality, religious, and other kinds of diversity currently exist among the people in the school as a whole? In lower, upper, middle school? In the various departments? Among students, faculty, administrators, coaches, trustees, advisors, in-dorm supervisors, leaders of extracurricular activities, non-teaching staff? Among those considered school leaders, student and faculty? Among the

"troublemakers"? Among the "jocks," the "nerds," the "artsies"? Among the withdrawn, the "non-participants"?

No, the part that raised his hackles and lowered his morale was called, "How Others Have Done It." Here were "Five Detailed Case Histories on Innovative Schools," followed by "Information on Other Schools With Innovative Programs." What were these centers of innovation doing?

Here was a school in St. Louis where "Valuing Diversity" was the order of the day. At this innovative school, "'Appreciation of Diversity' is assessed on report cards." "Anti-bias and multicultural topics are infused by classroom and specialist teachers alike. (Some examples: 6th grade emphasis on African drumming...)" It said, "Walls are used to educate both children and adults who enter the building, showing child-created special projects from skin-color graphs by preschoolers to...4th graders' graphs of put-downs tallied in a half-hour of prime-time TV." Further, "Implementation of theory of multiple intelligences in program has occurred for the last nine years."

Hoping that one of the topics in at least one of the grades was "reading and writing," Mr. Jones gulped and turned the page. Here he came to a school in St. Paul whose monomania was "Conflict Resolution." The page-long article, written, like all the others, by the school itself, said that "all adults including....kitchen staff are trained in conflict resolution and serve as models of integrating a problem-solving approach to conflict...." and that "Parents are trained in the program...." Here was the ultimate extension of a school's mission, thought Mr. Jones: teach the parents, too!

Mr. Jones hurried on, past the school in remote Alaska which "uses the Japanese business concepts of Total Quality Management and Continuous Improvement Process (*kaizen*) to prepare students for making a difference in the world beyond school," and found himself reading about an Episcopal school in Indiana which had a "multi-pronged character-education program". Here the daily required chapel service was referred to as "a 'chapel' assembly." What was the reason for the quotation marks? Ah, yes: although religion classes were "part of the required curriculum at all levels," they were "non-doctrinal," and, of course, "inclusive, and respectful of diversity." Mr. Jones, whose eight years of pre-Vatican II parochial school and four years of Jesuit high school had been characterized by un-apostrophed chapels and extremely doctrinal religion courses, wondered what "non-doctrinal" religious instruction was like. He imagined that it was taught by a non-sectarian minister, or a Modern Churchman, those types made so famous by Evelyn Waugh.

Further on in this fascinating booklet Mr. Jones came to schools whose obsession was "diversity." One of these made a fetish of having its Preschool and Kindergarten students celebrate every possible ethnic holiday: "Rosh Hashanah, Diwali, Martin Luther King Day, Black History Month, and so on." Mr. Jones hoped that "and so on" included Armistice Day, Washington's Birthday, and Easter. (But then he recalled that, although Dr. King gets his own day, Washington has been lumped together with Lincoln on Presidents' Day.) A school in St. Louis—obviously a city which was a hotbed of innovation and progress—said this about itself: "Opportunities for parent interaction were initiated by a cultural reception hosted by the head of school, attended by parents dressed in their cultural attire and bringing appetizers featured in their native countries... ." By now Mr. Jones was reeling. This was a day school and so would have few if any foreign students or parents. What in heaven was the "cultural attire" of an American? Or his "native country?" Were Americans supposed to exhume their pasts and dress up as starving Irishmen, deported English criminals, or slaves? What did this all mean? Did these wonderful educational innovators want the United States to wind up like the Balkans? (Mr. Jones also wondered how many of the students in St. Louis knew who St. Louis was. Did the curriculum include anything on Louis IX of France?)

106

Finally, not without effort, Mr. Jones reached the end of the pamphlet. Here he found something surprising. Under the title "Conclusion: Making a Commitment," somebody at ESAU had slipped up and revealed the methods that the brilliant innovators were to use to accomplish their goals. Starting from the premise that massive changes, along the lunatic lines covered in the booklet, were a matter of course, to be favored by every right-thinking educator, the booklet advised these fine people to do, among other things, the following:

1. Don't bother to try to convince your opponents. ("....turning opponents into active supporters is unlikely to be cost-effective in terms of energy.")
2. Fob your opponents off with meaningless ceremonies. ("When instituting significant change, consider a ceremonial way or ways of celebrating but 'letting go' the positive features of the old....")
3. Don't keep everyone fully informed. ("Share both triumphs and disappointments, though not necessarily with the same people.")
4. Manipulate reactions to your own advantage. ("In some situations, it may be necessary to state explicitly that asking for feedback does not guarantee it will be followed. In most situations it is desirable to share with the community what the feedback was....") "In most situations" was priceless.
5. Of course, hire consultants. ("Consider calling in an outside facilitator.")

Mr. Jones put down the booklet feeling bewildered and anxious. What did it all mean? School, to him, was a place to learn those things which educated people need to know. It was not a place where a gang of intellectual thugs brainwashed children into accepting their political and social opinions, and did this while trumpeting the lie that they really wanted students to think for themselves. It was certainly not a place where students, even tiny ones in kindergarten, were made to feel self-conscious and "diverse" because of their ancestors, or their religion, or their skin-color as shown on a graph. Mr. Jones could recall no nation which was ever strengthened by division and separatism, but he knew of some which had collapsed because of them. The USA, surely, had astonished the world in making "one out of many." Why were some people intent on making many out of one?

Mr. Jones knew that over half of the incoming sophomores at SLA could not identify France on an outline map of Europe. He knew that some juniors, taking Algebra II, could not add 1/4 to 1/3. He knew that almost no students read books for pleasure. Surely, surely, the first task of schools was to change themselves so that people did not reach age seventeen without knowing things they should have learned by age twelve! Perhaps they should concentrate on that for a while and worry less about teaching conflict resolution to their kitchen staffs or African drumming to their sixth graders. Yet nowhere in the green booklet could Mr. Jones find a reference to regular academics. He supposed that the oracles and seers at ESAU assumed that all was well on the traditional academic front, and he wondered when, or if, they would ever get their heads out of...the clouds.

XXIV. ONWARD AND DOWNWARD

The hockey season proceeded apace, as did Asmodeus Clovenhoof's occult studies. In fact, unknown to the athletes, the two now went hand-in-hand. The chaplain had determined that his intervention was directly affecting the games. He had done this by a nefarious method: one Saturday, when SLA was playing a team with which it was evenly-matched, he had worked a spell in behalf of the other side. SLA had lost 4-2.

Father Clovenhoof had been ecstatic, and he determined to move on to higher planes of thaumaturgy. He contacted other magicians and obtained scarce materials: rare herbs, unusual types of blood. In his letters he styled himself the "Archmage Potentius." He started wearing a black cape lined with crimson velvet, held at the neck by a golden chain.

His colleagues looked on him with awe. He was so intelligent, so witty, and so weird. Two or three faculty took to visiting him for counselling about marital and other problems. The students were divided into those who admired him and those whom he terrified. His Bible classes were exploring the outermost limits of pagan cults, with students researching Ishtar and Thoth and Carthaginian child sacrifice. He assigned Flaubert's <u>Salammbô</u> as a course book.

His low, soft, clear voice and penetrating eyes mesmerized his classes as he described how Yaweh became for the Israelites a very convenient deity, on whom they could put the responsibility for all the naughty things they had done during their big land grab in Palestine. "But, in the cities of those nations which the Lord, your God, is giving you as your heritage, you shall not leave a single soul alive. Deuteronomy 20,16" he read to his classes. "You must doom them all—the Hethites, Amorrites, Chanaanites, Pherezites, Hevites, and Jebusites—as the Lord, your God, has commanded you. Deuteronomy 20, 17."

They spent a lot of time on the Book of Joshua ("Maceda, too, Joshua captured and put to the sword....leaving no survivors. Joshua 10, 28") and the Book of Judges ("Adonibezec fled. They set out in pursuit, and when they caught him, cut off his thumbs and his big toes. Judges 1,6.") He relished analyzing the horrific tale of Jael and Sisera in Judges 4. He covered the story of how Saul was abandoned by God because he had not obeyed Jehova's order: "Now therefore go and smite Amalec, and utterly destroy all that he hath. Spare him not, nor covet anything that is his, but slay both man and woman, child and suckling, ox and sheep, camel and ass. 1 Sam 15,3." (Saul had killed all the people but spared some of the animals, and also at first spared the king, Agag. Even after Saul tried to make amends by disposing of the fallen monarch ("And Samuel hewed him in pieces before the Lord in Galgal") still God condemned Saul to defeat, and thousands of Jews to death, at the hands of the Philistines.

"Now, is this Jehovah really any different from the sanguinary gods of the other peoples?" asked Father Clovenhoof. "And is not the God of the Old Testament also the God of the New?"

He scared some students out of their wits.

On the day a voodoo priest in Haiti sent him some powdered monkey skulls and a ritual dagger, Father Clovenhoof could not resist trying a new ceremony, whose purpose was to summon the spirit called Vash, who would reveal the names of power necessary to perform spells of astral migration. After fasting for three days, until the moon was waxing, he carefully drew a new magic circle and performed the ceremony, using as his guide the <u>Lemegeton,</u> a very old grimoire which had been reprinted by the Société de Rose-Croix in Paris. About twenty minutes into the incantations all the candles went out, the chicken blood disappeared from its bronze bowl, there was a flash of light, and Father Clovenhoof fainted.

He came to in darkness, feeling dazed and weak. He groped his way to the light cord. When he turned on the overhead bulb he saw that the room was in great disorder, with the table overturned and books all over the floor. As he was feeling himself carefully for broken bones, a soft but penetrating voice said, "Don't worry, you're OK."

Fr. Clovenhoof almost jumped out of his skin. Whirling around, he cried, "Who said that?"

"I did," said the voice; and now the priest saw a jet-black pigeon perched on the top shelf of the recessed bookcase.

Fr. Clovenhoof stared at it. "Oh God, I'm going crazy," he muttered.

"No you're not," said the bird. "At least not yet. I'm Garbog."

"Who....what are you?"

"I'm your familiar, dumbbell."

The bird flew down and perched on an overturned chair. "Your spell penetrated to the lower aetherial plane. You almost summoned Vash—just as well you didn't. You have reached the level of Adeptus Minor, and you've got me now—whether you like it or not." The bird laughed, a strange peeping sound.

Fr. Clovenhoof slowly got up, wiping his brow with his sleeve. "A familiar? You're....you're a spirit?"

"Well I'm sure in hell not an ordinary pigeon, am I? Yes, I'm an aetherial entity from the ninth emanation of the Sephiroth. You know: Yesod, the Foundation, sun, stars, world in the major arcana of the Tarot? I'll give you advice and answer your questions and help you and guide you and try to keep you from killing yourself, which is what you're going to do if you keep meddling with spells like the one you just tried. You're getting in over your head, buster. But hey, don't worry, you're my master now. We'll be great together."

Fr. Clovenhoof was half afraid and half elated. His own familiar! A being from another plane of existence! He opened the door and staggered towards the kitchen. The bird fluttered after him.

"Er, would you like something to eat, Garbog? I need a sandwich."

The bird landed on the refrigerator. "Yes, cereal would be nice. And please make a nest out of some cloth and put it in a box. I've got to have some place to call my own."

While they ate, Fr. Clovenhoof regarded the pigeon warily. Exhilarated as he was by his advancement in the arcane arts, he was anxious about this unexpected development as well as by his failure to summon Vash. He asked Garbog what had not worked.

"Wrong words in the pentagram," said the familiar, between pecks at the dry cereal. "Adonai Tetragrammaton don't cut any ice with a demon as strong as Vash. Should have been Elohim Yod He Vau He, plus a pentagram of Solomon inside the circle. A couple of black cats wouldn't have hurt, either. Never mind. The circle held anyway. If it hadn't, they could put your remains in a thimble. But look, don't be too upset. Just by penetrating that high, you got me. Next time you'll do better. But you'd better take some time off, and not try spells that strong for a long time."

"But there are two hockey games this week. Can I still influence them?"

Garbog laughed again. "Oh, sure. That doesn't need anything too strong. What does it take to move the minds of hockey players? That's kiddie magic."

XXV. ROD THE GOD

The last faculty meeting before Christmas break was to be special. Instead of the usual agenda, the school's consultants would address the faculty on the current state of their plans for improving the place. The prospect of hearing from Broad Horizons, Inc., did not excite the teachers to any jubilation. By now almost everyone was sick of Dr. Rodney L. Glennis and his accomplices. They were paid vast sums—not that the faculty was ever told how much, of course—and what they seemed to do all the time was denigrate the school and suggest changes which were at best impractical and at worst ridiculous. They had thought up "athletic enhancement," i.e., the gigantic hockey program. They scorned academics. They didn't dare tackle Otto Auswurf's domain. But their every word was received by the administration like the pronouncements of an infallible seer. Some faculty wag had dubbed Glennis "Rod the God," and the name had stuck.

At the meeting, the great consultant outdid himself. Flanked by two associates, Drs. Helen Renna and Michael Featherstone—more Ed.D.'s—and surrounded by the usual farrago of charts, displays, blurbs, handouts, and overhead projectors, education's equivalent of the Delphic oracle revealed the latest mysteries to the uninitiated.

Dr. Glennis explained how, at their offices in Hartford, Broad Horizons had developed a "Future Greatness Plan" (FGP) just for St. Lawrence Academy. And what a plan!

"After three months of examining every aspect of SLA, we have concluded that, indeed, this place is still too bland, too blah, too plain vanilla," he declared. "All you have is excellent academics and a truly dedicated corps of fine teachers. Every school claims to have that. It's as common as dirt! You need things to make you special, unique. Your wonderful hockey program is a big step in that direction. It has helped to put you on the map." He beamed at Lance Vance, who beamed back.

"Now it's time to move into high gear." Dr. Glennis dashed to a tripod and uncovered the gaudy chart thereon while Dr. Renna scurried to turn on an overhead projector and Dr. Featherstone rushed to hand out an expensive brochure. And Rod the God spoke from Olympus.

Next year the first week of school would not be a week of regular, normal, stultifying classes. No. It would be....Adventure Academy. School would not begin "horizontally," it would take off, like a rocket, vertically. Vertical Week! There would be field trips galore, sensitivity groups, bonding experiences, mini-seminars, "lecturettes" in meaningful contemporary problems, like AIDS and drugs. The faculty would attend in-services on the seven types of learning, the functioning of the adolescent brain, and non-coercive discipline. Then classes would begin, but after four weeks the school would close and everyone would go off to the school's northern lake property for a "Wilderness Week" of camping, during which all would "attune with nature" and become "ecologically aware." (The hockey team, however, would remain behind to practice.) The week before Christmas vacation would be devoted to preparing and performing a "Boar's Head Festival," to which the whole town could be invited. There would be singers and dancers, jesters and mummers, revelry and feasting throughout Laud Hall.

On he went. Throughout the year whole days would be set aside to hold this seminar or that celebration. "On May 1 you'll recreate Merrymount and dance about the Maypole upon the green. Think of the publicity, as well as the kinesthetic value to poor adolescents cooped up in primitive, obsolescent 'classrooms'. The World is your classroom!"

The teachers gaped at him, mentally calculating what would happen to their courses if they lost over three whole weeks of time. Their minds boggled at the thought of the difficulties—

114

logistical, disciplinary, and personal—of a camping trip for over 200 people. Was this man serious?

Of course he was. Dr. Dukesbury sat there eating it all up: Dr. Glennis and some of his top aides had privately worked on him, and the other administrators, for several days before this presentation.

When Dr. Glennis paused for breath, Mr. Jones was bold enough to raise his hand and ask a question: "It seems that you are advising us to try to attract students by every possible means except by academics. What about getting students whose main reason for coming to this school, which is after all supposed to be a selective, college-preparatory institution, is because they want to work hard, learn a lot, and be well-prepared for college?"

Dr. Glennis just stared at Mr. Jones with blank incomprehension until Dr. Renna said to him, "I think he means U.M.'s, sir." Then Dr. Glennis's countenance cleared at once. He smiled and said,

"Ah, yes, of course. You mean attracting students by the strength of the academic program, especially in traditional areas such as English, History, and Mathematics?"

Mr. Jones nodded agreement.

"Students to whom such things appeal are quite rare and constitute only a small niche market. One might call them a boutique item. Targeting them is not cost-effective. Their demographic in this country is, what... .9%? Furthermore they tend to demonstrate what can only be called aberrant behavior for American teen-agers. They respect teachers and want to please them. They participate only in casual co-curriculars like tennis or fencing, or, or even, um, *chess*." He giggled. "They spend a lot of time reading books not required for classes, sometimes even big thick ones like <u>Anna Karenina</u> or <u>The Rise and Fall of the Third Reich</u>. They often write for pleasure, or collect things, like coins or stamps, or play musical instruments, or sometimes, well, just sort of sit and think. We call them U.M.'s, for Unsocialized Monomaniacs. They fail to take advantage of the wonderful smorgasbord of activities offered at good institutions. They are fixated on classes and learning things."

Dr. Glennis took a sip of water and went on. "The peculiar conduct of U.M.'s doesn't really help their chances for college, since, as I'm sure you all know, most U.S. colleges tend to prefer a B/C student who has some good sports and co-curriculars on their record, to some bookish recluses. U.M.'s are sort of, well, un-American. Of course every school has some, and it's part of your job to lead them from their myopic preoccupation with reading and learning and thinking into a spirit of full participation in the wonderful, enriching, life-enhancing variety of adventurous activities which your school offers—or will offer, when I'm done with it. Does that answer your question?"

"Yes," said Mr. Jones. "Unfortunately, it does."

Although this meeting seemed to last longer than the Council of Trent, it finally ended. (They all do, if you wait long enough.) Despite the startling nature of Rod the God's announcements, there was very little discussion among the faculty because it was 7:55. The on-duty housemasters rushed to their dorms, hoping that the students had not set fire to them in their absence; the duty master dashed upstairs to his gathering ESSH, and most of the others had papers to grade and classes to prepare before collapsing in bed. But a few people gathered at the back of the room, muttering together: Mr. Glover, the veteran English chairman; Ms. Green and Mr. Jones, historians; Ms. Ashton, who taught French.

"This is going to ruin us," said Mr. Glover softly, so that Dr. Glennis, who was still in the room, couldn't hear. "This is the craziest nonsense I've ever heard."

"He's going to turn us into a laughingstock," said Ms. Green. "We've got to do something."

"What can we do if the Headmaster supports it?" asked Mr. Jones. "This isn't a democracy."

"Of course we weren't consulted," said Ms. Ashton. "They never bother to ask us about these brainstorms."

The four teachers spoke together in impotent frustration for a few minutes more, until they were joined by George Fong, the Director of Studies. They all turned on him, berating the administration for going along with Dr. Glennis's mad schemes.

"Hey, don't blame me," said George, glancing around to see that the room was now otherwise empty. "Dr. Dukesbury is the one whom Glennis has mesmerized. And we're contracted to Broad Horizons for two more years—as long as they exist, we may as well get something for the money we're paying them." He left.

"We have to do something," said Mr. Jones. "I don't know what, but we have to. Think about it, folks, and let's meet after vacation. Adventure Academy. Vertical Week. Good God."

Outside Laud Hall the three consultants were getting into their rented Lincoln for the drive to the airport. Tomorrow they would be flying to New Orleans to start working their magic on a school there.

"Well, how do you think it went?" asked Dr. Glennis, pouring himself a well-needed shot of Scotch from his flask.

Dr. Renna, who was driving, said, "I think all this may be a bit radical for a traditional, stick-in-the-mud place like this one, boss. The teachers won't support it very well."

"I tend to agree with Helen," said Dr. Featherstone. "Is this really a good place to initiate the Adventure Academy and all-school field trip schemes?"

"Well, we have to start them somewhere," said Dr. Glennis. "You never know if these things will work until they're tried out under field conditions. This school is small and fairly remote. If it collapses, no one will notice. Besides we've got this Headmaster eating out of our hand. Not all of them are this tractable."

"That's true," said Dr. Renna. "We really dominate."

"Yes," said Dr. Glennis. "In fact, seeing that we have this place pretty much in our pocket, I think we should expand our plans for it by one more level. Paul, when we get back to Hartford, get in touch with our Gender Equity Task Force and

117

our Diversity Associates. Yes, we'll give SLA the <u>full</u> <u>treatment</u> at our next presentation."

"You mean....the Amazon?" asked Dr. Featherstone, with a catch in his voice.

"I certainly do," said Dr. Glennis with a smile.

The three great consultants sped off into the night.

XXVI. NOEL, NOEL, LET'S EAT IN HELL

SLA held its annual Chapel and Dinner on the evening of the last class day before Christmas vacation began. Chapel was at 6:00. Father Clovenhoof, constrained by the church calendar, could only stage an Advent service, but his sermon did identify Santa Claus with Morduck, the Chaldean weather god, and he drew parallels between the Roman festival of Sol Invictus, the Unconquered Sun, celebrated on December 25, with the Christian festival which replaced it. And there was a lot of incense.

Then everyone filed over to the refectory for the Christmas feast. The huge room was full to bursting, since all the parents had been invited and over fifty couples came. There was assigned seating, and tables normally holding seven or eight people now had ten or eleven.

There was a certain amount of drill and ceremonies before the meal. These traditions had mostly been taken over from Miss Pettipaw's Lyceum when it merged with SLA, and included a procession of wassailers, an appearance by King Wenceslaus, a visit from Santa, a couple of inspirational readings, and several toasts. After all this the student waiters went to the kitchen to get the delicious food—for which, by now, everyone was eager.

The tables were festively set with white cloths and red candles. There were paper cups of nuts and mints at each place, and a plastic cup of red juice which was unidentifiable before you tasted it, and also after. Everyone was in a good mood, hungry and anticipating a splendid repast.

Mr. Jones's table comprised nine other people, including a married couple and their daughter. These last were Mr. H. Smithfield Hamm, Ms. Beverly Townsend, and Miss Hilary Townsend-Pratt. (Mr. Hamm had divorced his first wife to marry Ms. Townsend. She had divorced a Mr. Pratt and retained custody of her daughter Hilary while deciding to revert to using her maiden name and to add it to her daughter's legal one. A typical boarding school couple.) The Hamms (if one can call them just that) were wealthy attorneys, and Hilary was a bright sophomore.

Mr. Jones, whom one could accuse of being a terrible pessimist and cynic, except that his negativity was so often justified, was at his witty best while trying to stifle a feeling of impending doom which had been growing ever since he had taken a sip of the dingleberry juice, or whatever it was. As the big double doors of the kitchen swung open and the waiters rolled the food carts into the hall—one cart for two tables—Mr. Jones gasped and muttered, "Oh, no."

On the carts were oblong rolls of bright and shiny tinfoil containing....what?

"It can't be," murmured Mr. Vetter, at the next table, to Mr. Jones. "He wouldn't dare serve that today, of all days."

The waiter brought the big platter to Mr. Jones. The teacher began peeling back the tinfoil, saying as he did so, "I feel like I'm opening Pandora's Box." And yes, there it was, before his very eyes: mulatto turkey. He beheld a tube of gray-brown meat, sparkling with grease, cut into slabs about an inch thick, resting on a bed, or, rather, mired in a swamp, of half-cooked stuffing whose main ingredient appeared to the eye, and to the nose, to be onions.

Accompanying this monstrosity was a bowl of broccoli greener than any broccoli should ever be, a bowl of gravy coated with a layer of congealed scum so thick that a heavy spoon could rest on it without sinking, potatoes like white mud, and some cement-like rolls.

Mr. Jones looked at Hilary's parents with a pained smile. "Well, I guess I won't have to ask if you prefer white or dark meat," he said as he took the serving fork in one hand and a plate in another. "It's, er, fully integrated."

As the feast progressed, gloom descended on the hitherto merry throng. This "turkey"—and God alone knows what

120

arcane rites were used to produce it, what processes unknown even to Upton Sinclair manufactured gray and blue-black meat—was awful. The stuffing was awful. The vegetables were awful. The whole meal was awful.

This refuse was served about once a month, on Sundays, but to send it out to guests, to parents, was incredible. It was an insult. Mr. Jones sat there watching the Hamms politely trying to force down food which at home they would not have fed to their Pekinese.

All through the hall people were sighing, complaining, giving up. Greg Stesson, a bright freshman at Joe Spofford's table, noisily dropped his fork on his plate and said, "This is garbage."

"Now, Greg," said Joe, tongue-in-cheek, "remember the starving people in Ethiopia."

"I'd rather starve than be poisoned," returned Greg, and the whole table laughed.

Then came dessert: plates of Special-K bars. It was the coup de grâce.

As the waiters started clearing the tables, Otto Auswurf appeared at the doors of the kitchen. The Food Service Manager was attired in immaculate white, complete with a tall chef's cap. And he was smiling, smiling as though to express the pleasure he felt in ruining a holiday and making 329 people miserable all at once.

"Otto, couldn't you do better than this?" asked George Fong, whose chair was next to the doors.

The tall, thin manager glanced down. His smile faded and was replaced by an angry sneer. "Hey, people were eating my food when you were a baby," he rasped, his prominent Adam's apple bobbing up and down. "Anyway," he continued with a chuckle, "it'll taste better tonight than it will in the stew after vacation."

He returned to his lair, unaware that three or four dozen people, including several teachers, covertly gave him the finger as he withdrew.

XXVII. THE SWORD OF JUSTICE

Christmas came and went and on January 4 school began again.

Two weeks into the new year Mr. Jones came home one Friday afternoon. He was tired, as usual, but greatly looking forward to the weekend. This was rare. What with doing duty, grading, prepping classes, chaperoning trips, driving vans, attending chapel, coaching sports, etc., etc., boarding school faculty do not really have the concept of a "weekend" which is shared by most other Americans. Not only is the famous expression "TGIF" largely meaningless at a boarding school, but every Friday about a third of the faculty are actually looking forward to Monday. However, as it happened, Mr. Jones had no duty and no grading to do this weekend, and his feelings were similar to those of a British soldier in 1916 who had been given leave to Blighty after the first week of the Somme.

At 4:30 the phone rang. It was Dean Rogers.

"I'm awfully sorry to have to bother you, John, but you're Rick Artamian's advisor, right?"

"Yes," said Mr. Jones, dreading what he knew was coming.

"Well, we've got a J.C. for Rick at 6:30 in the library conference room. Can you be there?"

"Yes, I guess so," said Mr. Jones. "What's up?"

"Quite a bit, unfortunately. About an hour ago Bill Vetter went over to the boys' dorm to see if Joe Spofford was in. He heard some girls' voices and investigated. Two boys and two girls were drinking beer in Jim Taylor's room. They had some liquor, too, and some marijuana, although they weren't smoking the pot."

"I suppose Rick was the other boy?"

"No. Two of the kids said that Rick is the one who sold them the stuff."

"Oh, great. OK, I'll be there."

Well, thought Mr. Jones as he hung up, that takes care of the evening. So much for listening to Gounod's <u>Faust</u>. He could be gone until ten or eleven.

J.C. stood for Judicial Committee. The Student Handbook said that in serious disciplinary cases the Dean would convene a J.C., at which would be present the student(s) accused, their advisors, the Dean, a proctor, and a member of the Student Council. They would investigate the matter and recommend action to the Headmaster.

John Jones cursed his luck in having Rick Artamian for an advisee. The boy was a new sophomore who had been assigned to him because—well, who knew why? Old students chose their advisors, but new ones were handed out by the Dean's office. Artamian was a small, shifty-eyed, sneaky boy, and Mr. Jones had not managed to establish much of a rapport with him. And now....well, the school looked on selling drugs as little better than murder, and there was no chance of Artamian remaining at SLA. To that extent, the J.C. was superfluous. Judicial Committees were normally held only when students had been caught <u>in flagrante</u>. They were not trials, since the defendants were regarded as already guilty. At best they could apportion blame, and discover extenuating cirsumstances. Mr. Jones recalled one occasion when, during a break from a J.C. which was investigating two students accused of possession of school keys, he had gone into the business office to discover, on the counter, the airplane tickets home for the two "defendants," already ordered by the school and charged to the parents.

The worst thing about J.C.'s was the fact that, with occasional exceptions, students never told the truth. They would lie about everything. They would deny obvious facts and things seen by several witnesses. Students caught with crib sheets would deny having used them. Students found with half-empty beer cans in their hands, or discovered puking into trash cans in the dormitory corridors, would deny drinking. Students confronted while staggering along a hallway, the pupils of their eyes the size of dinner plates, would deny using drugs. One freshman girl, found with three boys in a classroom one Saturday night, performing acts which even the veteran faculty discussed only in horrified whispers, denied knowing what she was doing. (The boys, all juniors, said they had been seduced.) It was depressing to see how completely SLA, and every other school, and most parents, failed in the basic mission of making people truthful and willing to accept responsibility for their actions.

The J.C. convened on time, presided over by Carl Rogers. Mr. Rogers. 46, had the toughest job in the school. The Dean of Students at a boarding school is responsible for everything which concerns students, outside of academics and athletics. A perfect dean would have to always know when to be gentle and when to be tough, be on-call twenty-four hours a day, know every student intimately, and would need a personality combining the salient features of Mother Theresa and Heinrich Himmler. Carl Rogers, a good-natured ex-Marine, did his impossible job as well as anyone could.

This J.C. was memorable, partly because of its length—it ended after midnight—and partly because some of the "accused" were willing to implicate another student, namely Rick Artamian. This was very rare, but one girl and one boy insisted that Rick had sold marijuana and some "reds" to her boyfriend. The boyfriend, however, denied it. Rick denied everything. Mr. Rogers sent two teachers to search Rick's room, and they returned with enough pills to start a small pharmacy. But then things got more involved. Confronted with these pills, Rick accused his roommate of hiding them in the room, and also accused another student of supplying the alcohol which had been present (two six-packs of beer and a fifth of peppermint schnapps, a ghastly potation which was for some reason a favorite with SLA's drinkers) Rick's roommate was absent on a free weekend, but this other boy was, as it happened, downstairs in the student lounge playing pinball. Mr. Jones was sent to get him, and the poor lad suddenly found himself on trial for his academic life (while his unfortunate advisor was summoned at a moment's notice to assist.)

Things became more and more complicated. The six students were isolated in separate classrooms, then brought in and re-questioned one by one. By 10:15 a spirit of investigative passion had taken possession of the seven faculty and two seniors conducting the inquiry. They sat on chairs in a circle, with the defendant on a hassock in the center of the ring having questions fired at him from all directions. Where did you really get the grass? The pills? The alcohol? Have you done this before? How often? Where? Paul said just the opposite, Mary—what's the truth? Really? OK, take Mary out and get Paul in here. OK, son, tell us again whose idea it was to skip sports and have a party instead. That's not what Rick said. What do you mean, you don't remember?

The final act came at 11:45. By now the scene reminded Mr. Jones of something out of the Spanish Inquisition. Rick Artamian was on the stand, or rather the hassock, and had repeated once more that the pills belonged to his roommate. Ms. Ellis, the advisor of one of the girls, glanced slyly at the Dean and said, "All right, Rick, now Mary and Rose both told us that you supply cocaine to some kids, but Jim says you only supply grass, and occasionally some reds. Which is it?"

And the tired, bewildered, frightened sixteen-year-old said, "Just some pills and weed. I never had nothing to do with coke."

And everyone grinned as Rick Artamian realized what he had just said.

"OK, Rick, that about settles it," said the Dean, covertly giving Ms. Ellis a thumbs-up sign. "But now tell us—*why* did you start selling drugs here? Why?" His voice became soothing and kindly. "You're not a bad kid. How come you'd do something like that?"

Rick, close to tears, muttered, "I borrowed $800 from my dad to buy an electric guitar. The deal was I'd pay him back in a year. I needed money to pay him."

"You....you needed," stammered Mr. Jones. "Do you....good lord, do you think your father is going to be happy when we tell him how his son has been earning money to repay him? When

125

he learns of that, that psychedelicatessen in your room? Don't you think that he would have <u>given</u> you the money rather than have you deal in drugs?"

"Yeah, I guess so," said Rick. "I was really dumb."

The festivities ended with the defendants being sent back to their dorms to await news of their fate, while the faculty and student members of the J.C. went into separate rooms to prepare their recommendations. This took about half an hour, and, as usual, the students were harsher than the teachers. The two seniors recommended dismissing everyone. The faculty were more discriminating.

It would have been highly embarrassing to have dismissed six students at once, and Rick Artamian's crime was far greater than those of the others. Therefore the decision was to get rid only of Artamian. The four students caught drinking were suspended at home for a week and put on social probation for the rest of the year. (The mandatory school punishment for using alcohol was suspension for the first offense and dismissal for the second, but use of drugs meant instant dismissal. Since the four students were not actually using the drugs they had, it was decided to overlook the marijuana and punish them only for drinking, and for unauthorized visitation.) The case against the boy whom Artamian had accused of supplying the alcohol was dropped for lack of conclusive proof, although the Dean did relieve him of a fake I.D. he found when he went through the boy's wallet. Rick Artamian's roommate was interrogated upon his return to campus and exonerated.

"Thank God you managed to get Artamian to admit what he did," said the Dean to Ms. Ellis.

"Yes, I'm glad that worked. Too bad I had to make up the part about the girls mentioning cocaine."

Next day the Headmaster routinely approved the sentences. The police were not informed about any of this—the Dean just flushed the drugs down the toilet—since the school did not want bad publicity, and because bringing in the civil authorities might have meant lawyers, lawsuits, and even annoying questions about "due process," "civil rights," school search procedures, and similar inconvenient things. Unlike public schools, SLA was not greatly concerned with students' "legal rights," preferring instead to consider itself <u>in loco parentis</u> for its boarders and thus justifying an approach to discipline which was sincere and caring but somewhat rough-and-ready. (The Dean's classic reply to the question from a new housemaster, "What does it take to search a student's room?" had been, "A master key.") Nonetheless these J.C.'s left a bad taste in one's mouth and most teachers wished the school could discover some less inquisitorial solution to serious infractions.

XXVIII. A LITTLE PROBLEM

It was a typical day in the midst of winter term. The Midwestern weather, capricious as usual, had been bitterly cold for several days but now had suddenly sent temperatures soaring to thirty degrees, granting a slight respite from the usual sub-zero conditions. But the north wind which swept across the flat, open campus, whirling about the powdery crystals of the five or six inches of snow which had covered everything since mid-November, put the wind chill down to five degrees, and there would be no real thaw until late March, if then.

Out at the arena Lance Vance was conducting practice for a team whose skills were now honed, like its skates, to a razor's edge. Their record was 28-3-2 so far, and on the coming weekend they were flying away for two games against a really tough opponent.

Lance smiled as he saw Simeon Affenkopf, his star forward, scatter his opponents like chaff before a gale as he burst through them and sent the puck deep into the net. As Simeon came off the ice Lance praised him and gave him a banana. Lance clapped his main goalie, Gus ("Bubba") Armstrong on the shoulder as the hulking junior passed, his knuckles almost touching the floor. He gave some quiet advice to Slobodan Mrgk, who had come to SLA from a far-away Slavic land with a national vowel shortage, and now served in the key position of the team's designated thug. He helped two of his younger players sharpen their skates until he was satisfied that they could, if properly used, sever an opponent's femoral artery or Achilles' tendon.

Lance loved his work, and as he stood at one end of the rink, next to the new Zamboni which had cost the school $67,000, watching the whole team go through a final drill, he felt a thrill of excitement, like Attila the Hun surveying his horde before unleashing it on the civilized West.

In the boys' dorm it was approaching study hall, but there was still time for a freshman who had made the mistake of being small and weak and Asian to be forced into a bathroom by two older boys and given a swirly, while a third bully kept watch for a housemaster or proctor. As Chuck and Pete pushed Nakasune's head into the toilet bowl and repeatedly flushed it, one said, "We're bein' too nice. Shoulda given him a dirty swirly instead of a clean one."

In the girls' dorm the Hockey Cheerleaders were in the lounge practicing a new routine. These girls were a new type of student at SLA, one seldom seen before. In recent years cheerleading had almost died out because the girls interested in athletics wanted to play sports, not to serve as cheesecake at boys' games. But the advent of the hockey program had somehow brought with it a number of females reminiscent of Boopsie in the early Doonesbury cartoons. These lovely and perfectly nice young persons seemed to find fulfillment in being seen with athletes, hanging on their boyfriends' arms and basking in the reflected glow of the stickmen's glory. Their performances at games were always welcomed by the crowds, for, owing to the fact that none of them could actually skate, they were often funnier than the clowns at a circus.

Amidst all these academic activities, in the bowels of Laud Hall, the Development Director was holding an emergency meeting behind the locked doors of his office.

Mario Pestalozzi sat at his desk, a look of astonished horror on his face, while his three main consultants, having just delivered their alarming report, sat before him, embarrassed and upset.

"But, God a'mighty," exclaimed Mario. "I can't believe you'd try something like <u>that</u>!"

"It wasn't us," protested Alfredo Ricci, whose corpulent form testified to a lifelong love of pasta. "It was that kid they sent to help us, Seamus O'Herlihy. He was in his early twenties and anxious to make a name for himself."

"Yes," put in Michele Garbandoni, "like Knuckles, I mean Roberto, said, we went to see this guy Orgule and we really had to lean on him just to get in when he finds out we're from SLA. Then Roberto makes his spiel and Orgule says get lost, so Boom-Boom, I mean Alfredo, starts out with the 'nice house you got here—too bad if it burned down' routine while Roberto gets out a donor form and I disconnect the phone and take out my shiv and this O'Herlihy kid stands by the door in case the maid comes in."

"And he signed up OK," continued Roberto Mazzarucci, "for $25,000 a year, but he obviously wasn't intimidated nearly enough and we thought we'd have to pay him a reminder visit before we left the state. But that night O'Herlihy goes back on his own and tries to burgle the wall safe that Orgule had shown us when he went to get his checkbook. The kid figures he can make us some extra dough. And, well, like I said, he sets off an alarm and he gets away, but not before Orgule gets a look at him. Orgule's so mad he calls the cops and then calls us to say that as soon as O'Herlihy is caught he'll have us all behind bars."

"Of course O'Herlihy won't be caught," said Mario.

"Not unless they drag the harbor," said Alfredo. "We took care of that idiot."

"No loss. What in hell is a Mick doin' in the Family anyway?"

"The Family's becoming an Affirmative Action Employer," said Roberto. "There's a twenty per cent quota for non-paisani now."

"We have to do something about Orgule," said Mario. "Even without O'Herlihy, the cops could cause us some trouble if Orgule's story gets them to start investigating our fund-raising methods."

"You want we should....," began Michele

"No," said Mario. "Not yet, anyway. I'm going to try something else. I'm going to ask for help from Above."

"You mean....Don Benito?" asked Alfredo.

"No, I mean our chaplain. The hockey coach was telling me this guy is really good at getting prayers answered."

The three men looked at Mario oddly, but this was his show, and they never questioned superiors. "Then we'll go out to Washington and work on, I mean with some alumnis there?"

"Right. And if this Orgule business isn't settled soon, I'll be in touch. The cops should be busy looking for O'Herlihy for a while."

XXIX. IN CASE OF AN ACCIDENT, PLEASE CALL A PRIEST

In the weeks since he had acquired his familiar, Father Clovenhoof had made as much progress in his exploration of the occult as in all his previous years. Garbog proved to be a faithful companion and skillful guide. Under his tutelage the priest had explored new parts of the Kabala, made progress in astrology, and spent a lot of time with the Tarot.

But Garbog advised his master not to cast spells. "It's the most dangerous thing you can do," he said, perched on the high back of the cleric's chair. "You can never be sure what will happen when you open a channel to the other planes. You found that out already, didn't you?"

"But the spells to help the hockey team went well, very well," protested Fr. Clovenhoof, who had come to enjoy the power he felt when he summoned spirits.

"Yes, master, but those spells were very simple ones and the SLA team was probably going to win most of those games anyway."

"But what about that second game in Milwaukee? That one was against a stronger team, and I used a more powerful spell than before."

"Yes. I admit that one went well. Karogadox did as you bade. But one swallow doesn't make a meal. Beginner's luck. You make a habit out of conjuring before you master lots of other things and you'll live to regret it—or maybe you won't live at all. Hey, can I have some food? Pigeon metabolism is pretty high."

Asmodeus Clovenhoof listened to his familiar and stopped casting spells for a while. He found that he slept better and felt healthier. But then came a day when Coach Vance visited him and implored his "prayers" for the big games in Medicine Hat.

"This tourney is really crucial," he said. "There'll be a lot of college scouts there. It would be great if the team could really shine."

"Great for players who might get 'scholarships?' smiled Fr. Clovenhoof.

"Yes, and good for me, too, if I get offered a college coaching job."

Fr. Clovenhoof promised to help, and Lance Vance left, all smiles.

Garbog, who hid behind a bookcase when his master had visitors, had heard all this. He now emerged.

"Are you actually going to help this guy?"

"Of course. I've done it before."

"Master, listen: SLA is slated to lose these games. Lose them bad, like 5-1 and 4-0. If you try to change that you'll have to use some big-time stuff. You'd better...."

The doorbell rang; Garbog disappeared behind the bookcase.

The caller was Mario Pestalozzi, and soon the burly man was seated on the sofa, his hands clasped between his knees and his whole attitude so forlorn that the chaplain thought the Development Director had come to go to confession. (Fr. Clovenhoof, like some other High Church clergy, "heard confessions," just as he "said Mass.")

"Father, I got a big problem," Mario began. "I hope you can help me."

"A priest of God is here only to serve," said Asmodeus with a smile, raising his right hand in a benevolent blessing.

Mario haltingly explained as much of his difficulty as he wanted the chaplain to know. He told how one of the school consultants had been overzealous in his duties and had offended a wealthy alumnus, and how this alumnus, Mr. Orgule, could cause a lot of trouble.

The phone rang. Fr. Clovenhoof answered it and handed it to Mario.

Mario spoke briefly. When he hung up, his face was ashen.

"That was my associate Mr. Mazzarucci. My wife told him I was here. Earlier today a warrant was issued for a Mr. O'Herlihy, our hasty colleague. Apparently they want him for a number of things. Oh, father, you've gotta help me. None of what happened is my fault, and this job is my big chance to turn over a new leaf. Father, can you use your, uh, powers of prayer to get Mr. Orgule to drop his charges and just sort of forget about the whole incident? No harm was done to him. The police aren't going to find Mr. O'Herlihy, so if Orgule drops his accusations, the whole thing will blow over."

Fr. Clovenhoof was not stupid, and it was apparent to him that Mario had been engaged in some sort of illegal activity. But the chaplain had great sympathy for anyone who came to him as a suppliant, and he saw no reason not to help a man who had done so much good for the school. Further, he was being asked to control someone's mind temporarily, and this sort of experiment was most appealing and exciting to him. And yet another reason to help Mario also appeared.

Mario took out his checkbook and said, "By the way, father, I've been meaning to tell you how much I admire your work here. Your sermons are very inspiring and much more interesting than the ones my family heard back in Chicago at St. Theresa of the Little Flower. I hope you can use a few pennies for your charities." He handed the priest a check for $9,000. "All I ask is your prayers."

Fr. Clovenhoof smiled. "Why, thank you, Mario," he said. He rose and put a comforting hand on his distressed colleague's shoulder. "I'll do all I can to help you in your hour of need." He escorted the grateful Development Director to the door.

Fr. Clovenhoof, deep in thought, turned and went to the bookcase in his study. Garbog fluttered into the room soon after. "Are you going to help him, too?" he asked.

"Yes," said Asmodeus. He took down a massive book, the oldest in his collection, and, using both hands, carried it to his desk. "Yes, I am. The time has come—I feel it in me—to rise to new heights. These two seekers coming at once are clearly an omen." He smiled with pride as he opened the tome. "I shall invoke the aid of Lucifuge Rofocale, Archduke of the Nether Pit and Vizier of Demons."

Garbog gave a terrific squawk and flapped his wings, flying erratically around the room.

"You can't be serious," he cried. "You're kidding—say you're kidding. Lucifuge Rofocale! Are you out of your mind? You could....you could level this whole campus if something went wrong." He came to rest on the desk.

Fr. Clovenhoof smiled indulgently at his excited familiar. "My dear Garbog, you underestimate me. You even underestimate yourself, for you have taught me much. Didn't you see how humbly those poor souls implored my aid? No, Garbog, the time has come for the Archmage Potentius to assert all his powers. I feel it in me!" He stood with one hand on the open book and struck an attitude, gazing into the distance, a confident smile on his face.

Garbog fluttered to the tripod in the corner. "Master, you're out of it," he exclaimed. "You're an Adeptus Minor, just barely. Even an Adeptus Exemptus would hesitate to approach Lucifuge Rofocale. You ought to be a Magister Templi before you even think about trying such a spell."

"Do not belittle my powers, famulus," replied the mage. "The moon is waning, and we will soon invoke the spirits."

"Couldn't you stick to Tarot cards for a while? How about the I Ching? They're so safe."

"Safety cannot be the main concern of adepts blessed with superior powers."

"Oh, great Thoth. Master, maybe you should go back to the Bible for a bit. You know, Proverbs 16:18? Pride is a cardinal sin, you know."

"Worry not, my dear spirit. Do not fear. You will be safe with me beside you." He closed the book, and, still smiling, went to say his bedtime prayers.

XXX. BACK IN THE TRENCHES

A Monday morning in February, 10:35 AM. Mr. Jones watched his Modern Europe Section 3, nineteen students, come into the room.

By now Napoleon had come and gone, right on schedule, and the course was in the gray, uninspiring Metternich era, 1815-1848, the period of European-wide repression: Ferdinand VII, Nicholas I, the Corn Laws, the Six Acts, George IV, Castlereagh, and suspension of habeas corpus.

Mr. Jones liked to think of this period as "Napoleon's Revenge": after so many years of fighting the Emperor and the revolution which he represented (at least in their minds), the people of England, Austria, Spain, Russia, and the other Coalition countries now received the thanks of their grateful rulers: the Peterloo Massacre, the Law of Compensation, and the Carlsbad Decrees. The English, in particular, got it in the neck, and in reading Shelley's 1819 to the class the teacher hoped to capture the spirit of despair which took hold of the freedom-loving people of Britain caught in the clutches of the odious squirearchy. The Gag Laws were such a nice reward for Waterloo.

As he went to shut the classroom door Mr. Jones was assailed by a terrible odor, an odor of greasy smoke so strong as to be almost palpable.

"Good lord," he said, turning towards the class, "what's that?"

"The kitchen," said a boy. "It's stronger downstairs."

"But we're on the third floor," exclaimed Mr. Jones. He closed the door and went to his podium. "I guess Otto is fixing something really special for lunch today."

The class laughed. Little did they know.

Mr. Jones began by handing back the previous day's reading quizzes, pausing to congratulate one student for his third perfect score in a row.

"Yeah, I'm doing better on them since I found my book," said the boy.

"Well, I suppose that does help, Jim. Where did you find it?"

"On the floor of my room."

Mr. Jones didn't ask how many layers of excavation that discovery had required, but he wondered how often the housemasters did room inspections. Then he gave out the next day's assignment and started the class. Today there was a bit of comic relief in the dull oppression of post-Napoleonic Europe, since the topic was France, 1815-1830. Yes, those zany Bourbons were at it again. Those madcap monarchs whose family had provided so many countries with so many incompetents had now produced their pièce de résistance, Charles X. Stupider than his brothers (Louis XVI and XVIII), as reactionary as Ferdinand VII of Spain, as foolish as any Neapolitan Bourbon, here we have France's answer to James II of England, here we have another idiot who tears himself up by the roots and blows away in the wind. The Law of Compensation, the Law of Sacrilege, the ineffable Polignac ministry of purblind imbeciles who had not learned a thing from a quarter-century of revolution and exile—what a good lesson on the necessity of learning from the past.

The class went well. This section had a lot of old students (i.e., ones who had been at SLA for two or more years) and included four really bright ones. Janet, for instance, actually anticipated Mr. Jones's comparison of Charles X and James II.

These able scholars threw into sharper relief the half-dozen very weak ones, like Dirk and Kirk, two exceptionally dense hockey players, and Heather Muldoon, whose social reputation made the Empress Messalina seem like a cloistered nun. As he looked out over his class while he lectured, Mr. Jones saw the two jocks sitting there amidst their note-taking fellows, their big empty heads floating above the bent backs of the others like two large balloons. He wondered why science could not invent some steroids for the brain. You could take a pill and add inches to your biceps, so why not a pill to add some new ganglions to the cerebellum? A glass of water, a quick gulp, and, "Gee, sir, now I can tell you why French liberals agreed to accept Louis Philippe as King in 1830 instead of insisting on a republic." Heather was checking her lipstick in her compact. (Mr. Jones had called her in a week before, not for the first time, to discuss her failing grade. He had ended by telling her that she must really like his course, since she evidently planned to take it again next year. "History repeats itself," he had said, "and some people repeat history.")

With Charles X on his way to England and the Citizen King about to appear with Lafayette on the balcony of the Hôtel de Ville, the bell rang and the period ended. Next came assembly. An alumnus, Mr. Nofziger, had expressed an interest in addressing the student body on his successful career in accountancy. The administration always let wealthy alumni talk to the students because by thus feeding their egos the school put them in a mood for giving SLA money. Mr. Nofziger bored everyone to death—indeed, since his presentation was the fifth class in a row that morning, Demosthenes would not have been very effective—and then came lunch.

XXXI. JUST DESSERTS

The noxious odor which had penetrated to the third-floor classrooms had been even more noticeable in the auditorium, and as the school converged on the refectory it became appalling. The dining hall was in fact filled with a haze, and Mr. Glover remarked that today his cholesterol count might rise merely from breathing.

The teachers and students went to their assigned tables. The proctor on duty read Grace, and "bless this food to our use" sounded like a necessary appeal on this occasion The waiters went to the kitchens to get the food carts.

"What's on the menu?" Mr. Jones asked a student.

"Hamburgers," said the girl.

The waiters wheeled out the carts and brought the serving dishes to the tables. The plate of "hamburgers" which was put in front of Mr. Jones is hard to describe. The irregularly-shaped objects lying one upon another were dark gray, flecked with white blotches, and were floating in a morass of grease, awash in a swamp of oily liquid which reflected light made iridescent. There was also a bowl of almost solid white mud which was apparently supposed to be potatoes, and some green beans which had been boiled far beyond their capacity to be boiled and still be beans.

But the triumph of this meal was the onion rings, and when they arrived at the tables in oval bowls the origin of the stench which was by now making some people nauseous was revealed. They were vile and hideous: misshapen circles of pure grease the thickness of a small doughnut, steaming and giving off an odor like a gas grenade.

"Aaaah, take them away!" exclaimed Mr. Jones as the students at his table held their noses, averted their faces, and gasped for air. "Get them out of here." The waiter removed them to the cart.

Mr. Jones, aghast at this latest atrocity, began mechanically to serve the meal. He did not have much to do. Only four of the eight students wanted a "hamburger" and none would touch the potatoes or the beans. The waiter was sent for peanut butter and jelly.

Mr. Jones pressed his fork against the thing on his plate; it made a hissing noise and oozed a rancid, viscous fluid. He dared not eat it. He took a forkful of potatoes. As he raised it to his mouth the boy on his left gave a grunt of disgust and said, "The milk's sour again." A moment later Mr. Jones felt a crunch in his mouth as he bit on something very hard, and then he was staring at the piece of filling which the pellet of solidified fat in the potatoes had broken. His tongue probed the hole in his tooth. He felt no pain, but now he would have to get to a dentist quickly.

Mr. Jones was not a finicky man when it came to food. As a bachelor in middle age he was used to eating what he could get, and his own skill at cookery was limited to heating frozen dinners in a microwave. But this was too much. Something gave way in his well-disciplined mind and he was overcome with anger, like Cavour upon receiving word of the Villafranca agreement in 1859.

"Damn that stupid incompetent poisoner," he exclaimed. "We work hard all morning and we get fed swill, like pigs."

It was highly unusual for a teacher to use any harsh language in front of students, and today Mr. Jones's unprofessional solecism served as a catalyst for the feelings of those around him.

"We pay $20,000 a year and get garbage," said a girl.

"This food sucks totally," said a boy. Table Twelve was not alone in these sentiments. Far from it. The whole dining room seemed to be filling with mutterings and curses, grumblings and growlings, and then suddenly a voice rang out, loud and clear, from the north end of the big refectory: "To hell with this crap!"

No one ever knew for sure who raised that cry, but within seconds the dining hall resembled a battlefield. Driven beyond all endurance by years of bad food, the victims of Bonne Cuisine Inc. went temporarily mad. Platters of hamburgers hurtled through the air and crashed to the floor. Handfuls of potatoes flew towards the kitchen doors, adhering to them. Whole food carts were tipped over. The rock-hard doughnuts waiting for dessert made fine missiles.

And Mr. Jones yelled a war-cry, picked up a carton of sour milk, and hurled it as hard as he could towards the kitchen. Joe Spofford threw a bowl of beans into the air. About half of the faculty joined the food riot, and the others did nothing to stop it. The room resembled a bombardment in World War I as everything movable was thrown in arcs across the room.

This tumult naturally attracted the kitchen staff, who opened the big doors, and Otto Auswurf himself came out to see what was going on. He pushed his way into the dining hall. That was Otto's big mistake.

As soon as the berserk populace saw the Food Service Manager, attired as usual in spotless white, a cry of rage shook walls and ceiling. Several voices bellowed, "Kill the bastard!" and the crowd rushed towards the kitchen doors.

Otto Auswurf stood and stared, shocked beyond belief. Not Louis XVI in 1789, receiving word of the fall of the Bastille, not Charles X in today's Modern Europe lesson being notified of the July Revolution, could have been more amazed. Forty-one years of seniority had, he thought, placed him above accountability and beyond criticism. Now he saw his victims turning on him, hate in their hearts, murder in their eyes, and grease on their hands.

He turned and ran, through the gaping crowd of his subordinates, around the hot table, and towards the rear door. But the rear door was blocked by two burly men delivering a huge box of day-old bread, which Otto was planning to use next week for grilled-cheese sandwiches. As he tried to claw his way past this unexpected obstacle, Otto was grabbed by a couple of nimble freshmen, who had slipped, ferret-like, ahead of their fellows, and then by some brawny hockey players, who hoisted him aloft and passed him on to the mob now flooding into the kitchen. In a trice Otto Auswurf was being tossed about on a sea of hands, like a cork on the waves of an angry ocean.

"Stuff him into his fryers," called a voice above the general roar. "Turn him into a giant corn dog!" Cheers and shouts; Otto found himself moving towards the fry baskets.

"No, lock him in the freezer," yelled another voice. "See if he goes sour." Laughter and cries; Otto's helpless form moved through the air towards the walk-in refrigerator.

At the kitchen doors Ms. Green said to Mr. Jones, "John, we've got to do something. We can't let him be killed."

"Why not?" replied her colleague, conscious of his broken filling. "It would be no great loss."

"John!" exclaimed Ms. Green, pinching his arm.

Mr. Jones blinked his eyes and swallowed. "Oh, yes, I suppose you're right, Fiona. But you know, in 1672 the de Witt brothers, who ruled Holland, were torn to pieces in the streets by their own fellow-citizens, who blamed them for Holland's weakness in the face of Louis XIV's aggression. The same thing happened to the body of Marie de Medici's favorite, Concini, after her son, Louis XIII, had him shot. I've often wondered what being 'torn to pieces' looks like, and this would be a great chance to find out."

"Is this the time for a history lesson?" exclaimed Ms. Green.

"Everything we do is a history lesson," replied her colleague serenely.

By now the mob was debating whether to throw Otto Auswurf off the roof of Laud Hall or to carve him up with his own steak knives. Dean Rogers was frantically shouting from the back of the crowd—he couldn't get into the kitchen—for somebody to do something. Otto was whimpering in fear.

Mr. Jones climbed onto a counter. "I know what to do," he yelled. "Make him eat his own cooking. Put him on that table and feed him some of this garbage he gives us."

A yell of agreement went up and soon Otto Auswurf was spread-eagled on his back and a plate of the untouchable greaseburgers and ineffable onion things was brought up. Brawny arms raised the chef to a sitting position and a student waved a fetid onion ring in his face. "Eat it, eat it, Otto," cried the mob.

Otto shrank back. "I can't," he whispered. "I....I'm allergic to onions."

Then one of the kitchen staff spoke up. These people had at first huddled in a corner, afraid for their lives, as the mob stormed in. Now, seeing that the anger of the maddened proletariat was directed solely at their odious and tyrannical boss, they took courage. It was the Second Cook who said, "He never eats school food. Look in his office."

Several athletes tore the locked door off its hinges and entered the Food Service Manager's private office. They found a second door, which Bruto Grubnecker broke down with one kick. This revealed a room with a refrigerator, a stove, and a microwave. The refrigerator was filled with T-bone steaks, prime rib, salmon, and fresh vegetables. In the cupboards were gourmet condiments and other delicacies such as no one had ever seen at SLA. This discovery was carried through the kitchen by the excited shouts of the crowd.

"His wife comes up to make him supper," called out the pastry cook. "Last night he had lobster while he served you fried scrod."

A shriek of rage shook the refectory. An onion ring was stuffed into Otto's mouth, then another and another. His apron was torn off, and, together with his tall cap, trampled and stomped on by the students. A platter of hamburgers was dumped in his lap.

Mr. Jones, still atop the counter, looked down at Ms. Green. "During the Indian Mutiny in 1857 the British soldiers often punished rebellious sepoys by forcing them to eat pork, thus defiling them and breaking their caste. Then they hanged them. This may be an analogous case." Then the historian yelled, "Smother him in his own refuse and carry him to the bridge. Ride him out on a rail!"

The mob yelled in glee as Otto, half choking and turning green, was just drenched and submerged with anything that came to hand. They brought a bench, and the evil chef, made to straddle it, was hoisted aloft again. His hair was smeared with peanut butter, his spare body covered in gravy and salad dressing with potato chips and lettuce stuck to the oily mess. Mashed potatoes had been shoved down his pants, ketchup squirted over his chest, and his shoes had been torn off, filled with mustard and garbanzo beans, and forced back onto his feet.

The mob began to move, the terrified Otto clinging desperately to the bench while two hundred tongues reviled him and eager hands pelted him with his own petrified doughnuts. Through the refectory they went, down the main corridor, out the door, down the steps, and across the big lawn. Finally, arriving at the entrance, the howling multitude pitched the bench and Otto into the stream which ran below the little bridge and marked the border of SLA. Then, under a hail of insults and missiles, Otto Auswurf, bruised, battered, breathless, and scared to death, scrambled up the bank as best he could and ran away, across lawns and back yards, into the distance.

Dean Rogers climbed onto the parapet of the bridge. "OK. Enough," he yelled. "Afternoon classes are cancelled. We'll all clean up the dining hall. Break into advisor groups and report to me there. I'm sure that the Headmaster will be speaking to us all about this soon."

Back in the refectory, at High Table, Dr. Dukesbury was still sitting with his wife and the seven students who formed his group. They had sat there stunned, mute witnesses to the whole incredible scene. The Headmaster's coffee cup was still poised in his hand above the table. And Dr. Dukesbury, coming out of his shock, muttered, "I never dared to fire him, but now he's gone." He paused, looked at the food on his plate, and exclaimed, "Thank God!"

XXXII. THE QUALITY OF MERCY IS NOT FRIED

Next morning there was a special assembly at which the Headmaster addressed the school. Dr. Dukesbury had spent much of the previous evening in conference with the Dean of Students and the Director of Studies, trying to work out a response to what was being called the Food Rebellion. Now he stood at the podium before his teachers and students.

"After the events of yesterday," he began, "it's clear that we all need to process what we've been going through. I'm sure that a lot of ventilation has already transpired in the dorms, and more will eventuate. We must all strive to internalize the ramifications. I assume we can assume responsibility for our collective and individual actions and thus initiate ameliorization of any regrettable transgressions which happened to happen."

He paused and smiled. The students were encouraged by his smile, and that was good, because, as usual, they had not understood a word he had said.

"What many of you, students and faculty, did yesterday was ostensibly an unconstructive and inappropriate manner of dealing with a stressful situation, yet mitigations abound, I admit. In this unique instance, having considered all the true facts, and realizing that I must strive to have congruent anticipatory sets which match yours, I am inclined to assume a clemmical attitude to once again unite us in our common endeavors. Now I will ask the Dean to amplify the measures we will take. Rean Dodgers?"

Dean Rodgers spoke to the bewildered students. "We're declaring an amnesty for anything done at lunch. You're all forgiven. Otto Auswurf phoned in his resignation this morning. Bonne Cuisine is naming Mr. John Clark, the First Cook, as his successor. Mr. Clark has promised immediate improvements in the food. The school will be opening its contract to new bids for next year, and we've told Bonne Cuisine that they'll have to compete with other food services to retain our business."

Everyone understood that. The assembly ended with prolonged cheering.

XXXIII. IDOL CURIOSITY

Father Clovenhoof was unaware of the Food Rebellion because he was fasting when it took place. This fast was part of his extensive preparations for the Grand Conjuration, as he called it, to summon the demon Lucifuge Rofocale for the double purpose of assuring a victory for the hockey team in its tough Medicine Hat tournament and influencing Mr. Orgule, the refractory alumnus, to withdraw his charges against the Development Department.

There was a lot to do. The demon's *sigillum*, or magical sign, had to be drawn on virgin parchment with a silver pen after midnight under a waxing moon. A "salad" of several esoteric herbs had to be prepared to assist the summoning. The magical circle had to be drawn with a mixture of chalk, black ink, and mercury, and special names of power inscribed within its double rim. And so on. The ritual itself had to be carefully rehearsed, of course.

Throughout all this Garbog was as much of an annoyance to the Archmage Potentius as he was a help. The familiar harped on the dangers involved and tried to discourage the priest from his plan.

"You're really asking for it, master," he would say as he watched the man tracing the demon's sign on paper. "You're not ready for this. You're risking too much, and for what: a hockey team and some Mafiosi."

"They are not the prime reason," replied Asmodeus. "By gaining mastery over Lucifuge I will ascend to the fifth plane, will I not? I will attain access to the medium arcana."

"You may ascend a lot higher than that," said Garbog, fluttering down from the bookcase to land on Fr. Clovenhoof's desk and inspecting the diagram. "Those center lines should be red, not black. Why not stick to the Tarot for a while?"

147

"Do you doubt I can summon Lucifuge Rofocale?" asked the priest sternly.

The bird gave a few peeps of laughter. "Oh, no, master. I'm <u>sure</u> you can <u>summon</u> him. That's not what I'm afraid of."

"But...."

"What I'm not sure of is that you can <u>dismiss</u> him. You'll get old fly-the-light in your den and give him his orders and then you'll find he won't go away, and where will you be then? Look, if you must summon something bigger than usual, try Belphegor. He's nearly as powerful and much less risky."

"Your trepidations are groundless, my dear famulus," said the chaplain as he got up. "The dismissal ritual is clear and I have been practicing it." He turned the pages of his grimoire. "See, here it is, on page 774. Yes, tomorrow we will assert our mastery over the Vizier of Demons."

"Not tomorrow," said Garbog. "Neptune is still in Libra. You want him in Scorpio."

"Oh, yes, then the next night. That will be fine. All will be well, you'll see." He swept from the room, his cape billowing around him.

··················

At 10:30 on the appointed night Fr. Clovenhoof was in his conjuring chamber, wearing black robes and carrying his hazel wand. All was in readiness. The candles were lit, the brazier smoked, the <u>Grand Grimoire</u> was open on a lectern inside the magic circle. Garbog sat next to his master's feet, cooing nervously. "Last chance," he whispered. "You can still stop."

The mage ignored him and, raising his wand, began to read.

"In nomine Dei conjuro. Ego, Asmodeus Clovenhoof, Archimagistratus Potentissimus, secerti secretorum possessor, high priest of the Sephiroth, do command and summon the spirit Lucifuge Rofocale to serve my will."

He sprinkled henbane into the brazier.

"By the names ORMAGON, TISHABOND, VROOMCHUR, CROMATZ, I conjure and command you, spirit of darkness, to appear before me humbly and obediently."

Now he dipped his wand into a bowl of gray paste—it had taken three hours to compound the arcane contents of that bowl—and inscribed the seal of Lucifuge Rofocale on the floor. His voice rose. "In nominis KORBONDOLO, MAMARIPSON, FLAGAROTOBOLON, appear. Fiat! Fiat! Fiat!"

Father Clovenhoof began to feel fatigued. It was as though energy was being drained right out of him. He had never felt anything this severe before.

After delivering his triple "Fiat!," and nothing had happened, Fr. Clovenhoof held the spirit's parchment sigillum above his head with both hands and spoke the word 'ADOMATON!"

At once the house trembled slightly and there was a flash of crimson light in front of the priest, just outside the circle.

"Contact," said Garbog, who was now cowering behind the legs of the lectern.

And there, standing on the floor, was a leopard, very large and powerful, with huge fangs. And this apparition spoke in a low, angry growl.

"Mortal dog, why do you disturb me? What is thy desire?"

Father Clovenhoof was frightened. He was also exhausted, for the drain of his energy had doubled when the spirit appeared. For the moment, however, his fatigue took second place to his anxiety, for even within his protecting circle he could feel the hatred for him, and for all mortal beings, which emanated from the spectral leopard.

Perhaps another mage would have revelled in exercising power over so dangerous and contumacious a spirit, but Asmodeus Clovenhoof was not Aleister Crowley, even if he did have the same initials. He was a thinker and a dreamer. Magic and the occult fascinated him as an intellectual exercise and a scholarly pursuit. He now realized that the more active side of the Hermetic Art was not to his liking. However, this was not really the best time to acknowledge this discovery, not with a magical leopard sitting in the study and glaring at him with pure hatred. As they say, the wine had been drawn and had to be drunk.

Father Clovenhoof, responding to the spirit's question, stated his wishes, stumbling over some words and marvelling at the banality of his requests. Calling in Lucifuge Rofocale to fix a hockey tournament and give Charles Orgule amnesia seemed, to put it mildly, like overkill.

"Therefore obey my will, spirit of darkness," croaked the magician, who was by now draped over the podium and sweating profusely. The leopard stared at him and licked its fangs.

"Depart, begone," said Fr. Clovenhoof.

Nothing happened.

The priest barely had strength to raise his wand. "Depart, go, obey my will," he gasped.

The leopard moved closer to the circle. Its front paws touched the outer rim.

Garbog peered at his master from under a wing held over his face. "The word of power," he whispered. The priest seemed not to hear him. "The valedictory word," hissed Garbog more loudly.

The priest moaned. "I, I forget the page," he said as he tried to find the right place in the grimoire. "I....I...."

The leopard growled. Its left forepaw moved half way into the double outer rim of the circle.

"Page 774," said Garbog in a terrified squeak.

"Yes, yes, I have it now, I see it," whispered the magician. He opened his mouth and found he had no energy, no willpower, simply to say the word he saw before his eyes.

"Mortal dog, now come with me to Hell," growled Lucifuge Rofocale. Both his forepaws were almost across the lines on the floor.

Garbog gave a terrific cry and flew to the podium. "Aaaah, master, he's breaking the circle," he shrieked.

The leopard gathered itself to spring, and flashes of pale blue light appeared around its head. Another tremor shook the house.

Garbog hopped onto Fr. Clovenhoof's shoulder and gave the priest's neck a hard jab with his beak. The priest, jolted by the pain, shouted convulsively, "MARCOLOSAR!" as the leopard jumped. The beast roared and seemed to explode.......

....

Joe Spofford and his friend Paul del Rey, the housemasters on duty in the boys' dorm, had put their charges to bed and were taking a stroll around the campus just to get out in the air. They were joined by Dean Rogers, who was walking his dog. The three were about seventy-five yards from the chaplain's house when they saw light flash from behind a window, heard muted roars, and felt the ground shake slightly.

The three men looked at each other in alarm.

"You know, some students say that Fr. Clovenhoof is into casting spells," said Joe. "Do you think one went wrong?" He laughed.

"I think we'd better take a look," said the Dean.

They went to the front door. No one answered the bell. "We've got to go in," said Mr. Rogers, and they forced the door open.

The house was all dark. Joe Spofford finally found a light cord. They saw smoke curling along the corridor leading to the back part of the house, which grew thicker as they approached a door there. They rushed to it, flung it open, and stared into the dim interior. Mr. Rogers's dog began to bark excitedly.

In the center of the magic circle, behind the podium, was a heap of clothes. In the center of this heap, just crawling out from under it, was a large frog. It looked at the men and said, "Ribbit."

Again the three men exchanged glances. "I think Father C bit off more than he could chew," said Joe slowly.

Then they heard a voice. "It's a miracle he's alive at all. This should wear off in two or three days. Be sure to give him some flies. We dismissed Lucifuge but he had some revenge."

They looked up to see a large pigeon with a black head but with almost every feather ripped off its body perched atop a bookcase. "So long. I'm outta here. Tell the poor guy to stick to the Tarot." And the bird just vanished.

Paul del Rey fainted, quietly, on the rug. Joe and Carl turned on some more lights and carried their inert colleague to the living room, where they sat talking until he revived.

"I'll go see the Headmaster," said the Dean at last. "Can you, uh, take charge of, of Father Clovenhoof?"

Joe went to the room, glancing in astonishment at its magical appointments, and gingerly gathered up the frog, which was sitting disconsolately near the brazier.

XXXIV. THE REFORMATION

The next day there was a sign outside the academic office which read, "Father Clovenhoof's classes are cancelled today." At lunch the Headmaster stood up at High Table and read a brief announcement, which Dean Rogers had written out for him. "The chaplain has been unexpectedly called away. He should return soon. Mr. Fong will take his classes starting tomorrow, until Fr. Clovenhoof returns."

The three teachers who had discovered the chaplain's unfortunate transfiguration had decided to keep it a secret. Dr. Dukesbury did believe that the priest was out of town on a family emergency. Mr. del Rey, who taught biology, had taken the frog to his lab and put it in a glass case. One of the three men kept it under surveillance all weekend. On Sunday night Mr. del Rey took it to his home. A cleric from the Cathedral did Sunday chapel.

The results of the big hockey tourney were disappointing: SLA lost 5-1and 4-1, and two players were injured.

On Monday the FBI arrested Mr. Pestalozzi, who was charged with conspiracy, racketeering, and extortion. He was released on $200,000 bail, the money being posted by a Mr. Benito Bontucci in Chicago.

On Monday afternoon Mr. Del Rey came home to find Fr. Clovenhoof sitting in his living room, wearing some of the science teacher's clothes. Joe Spofford was talking with him. "He materialized a little after three," said Joe. "I had gone to the can and when I came back, there he was."

"Uh, how are you feeling, father?" asked Mr. Del Rey.

"Transformed," replied the priest with a rueful smile. "How many people know what happened?"

They told him that only three knew and readily agreed to permanent secrecy. "Ask me no questions," said the priest. "Nothing like this will ever, ever happen again."

That evening Mary Coster was walking across campus when she saw a big pile of things in the gravel driveway of the chaplain's cottage. She came over and saw that Fr. Clovenhoof had made a great heap of books and papers.

"Housecleaning, father?" she asked the man, who was adding more tomes to the pile.

"Yes," said the priest with a grin. "You could say that." He picked up a can of kerosene and began pouring it all over the books. "There's not too much wind, do you think?" Then he flicked a match onto the pile and watched as it caught fire. The snow began to melt as the flames spread, igniting the works of Papus, Eliphas Levi, and A.E. Waite, singing the <u>Arcana</u> of Vacaridius, fastening on the <u>Lemegeton</u> and the <u>Clavicle of Solomon</u>.

"Gee, father," said Mary, "those books look really old. Why are you burning them?"

"Because <u>I</u> want to have a chance to get really old," replied the priest, and he walked into his house smiling happily and humming "Give Me That Old Time Religion." He came back with a rake and used it to stir the flames.

"How are things with your boss?" he asked Ms. Coster.

Mary turned her fresh, innocent face towards Fr. Clovenhoof. "Oh, father, isn't this just awful? Mr. Pestalozzi is such a <u>nice</u> man, and he's done <u>so much</u> good for the school. I can't <u>believe</u> all those horrible charges against him are true. Even if the consultants did get a little carried away, that's not Mario's fault, is it? John and I are running Development because Mario is too depressed to come to the office. I hope you'll pray for him."

Father Clovenhoof pushed the <u>Black Pullet</u> deeper into the flames and said, "Oh, yes, I certainly will—but that's all I can do."

Shortly after Mary left, Lance Vance came driving by and stopped to chat. He was depressed, too. "Cripes, the team's all shot after that loss, and with Bruto and Simeon out for the season we'll be lucky to win another game."

"But isn't the season about over?" asked Fr. Clovenhoof.

"Hell no, not the way we play. I've got games lined up through the first week in April. We'll be playing right through winter finals and spring break. Geez, it's gonna be rough." But then a grin creased his handsome features. "Wait'll next year, though. Our road trips have been giving us great publicity and I been recruitin' like crazy. You should see some of the boys I got lined up for us next year. I got a kid from Los Alamos who's crippled three opponents so far this season, and a Canuck goalie they call the Great Wall, 'cause nothing gets past him. There's a sophomore from Milwaukee, Gurk Maimer, who gets so wild at games he has to be handcuffed to the bench when he's not playing. We got a great future!"

He drove off. Fr. Clovenhoof shook his head and raked some coals onto Aleister Crowley's novel, Moonchild.

XXXV. DREADFUL OMENS

It was the last week in February. John Jones, Violetta Ashton, Fiona Green, and Bill Glover sat disconsolately in the English teacher's living room. The four were meeting to discuss the latest bad news concerning Broad Horizons, Inc., the consulting firm which was doing such harm to the school. They sat sipping Coke while Mr. Glover's son played with his trains in the next room. They were going over the memo which everyone had received earlier in the day, announcing that next Monday evening there would be a special faculty meeting at which Dr. Glennis would present the revised final plans for "dynamising" the school in the next year, "including revolutionary innovations for energizing the Social Studies curriculum with cutting-edge courses in Sociology, Diversity, Multiculturalism, and Gender Studies."

The memo went on to say that Dr. Glennis would be accompanied by Dr. Channing Blither, the "chairperson" of the Department of Education at a famous university, and by Dr. Cynthia Mann-Hayter, the distinguished feminist whose most recent book, <u>Women Are From Heaven, Men Are From Hell</u>, had gained such favorable attention in the academic world.

"This is the end," said Bill Glover. "The end. These people can't even write English. What in hell does 'dynamising' mean?"

"It might as well be 'dynamiting,' said Violetta Ashton. "They're going to start meddling with the curriculum now."

"But I'm sure that Dr. Mann-Hayter will be most interesting," said Fiona Green, with a sly glance at her chairman. "Especially if she is going to advise us on Gender Studies and Diversity. Don't you think so, John?"

Mr. Jones was the most stricken of the group. He was staring into space as though stunned. He was almost physically allergic to the words "social studies" and the idea that his beloved History Department was about to experience the lethal grip of Rod the God and his evil associates was too much for him.

"Sociology," he muttered, pronouncing the word with loathing. "Multiculturalism. Gender Studies. No, no, never. We are not going to cut down, or eviscerate, our courses in American and European History—History, by God, not 'Social Studies,'—to add some trendy idiocies. What can we do?"

"That's what I wonder," said Violetta. "As long as the Headmaster is under the thumb of these people, we're going to follow their plans. We need a miracle."

There was a knock on the door. Bill answered it and in came Leo Carter, the Director of Admissions. "Hello, everybody." he said. "I came over to ask Bill if we could send a couple of prospectives to his period six class tomorrow."

"Yes, sure," said Mr. Glover. "And how are things?"

"Just great. That's another reason I came. We had some wonderful news today."

"Tell us," said Violetta. "We need some."

"Well, Mrs. Faraway's money came through. That's $1.6 million. And I managed to persuade Dr. Dukesbury to add to it another $1.1 million from all the dough that Mario has been bringing in. So the financial aid budget for next year has been quadrupled. Now we can really make an effort to admit lots of smart kids who can't afford full pay."

The four teachers chorused their delight, but Mr. Jones added, "What if the Hockey Department gets it? I'm sure that Lance knows lots of players swinging from trees by their tails whom he'd love to buy."

"No," said Leo. "That won't happen. You see, Hettie Faraway followed Mario's advice—which I helped to put into his head. It's really a little odd, I admit, sort of outlandish, in fact. But the idea is that her money would be restricted to students who are smart. It will be given only to those with high grades and SSAT scores. The concept is that a school like SLA, which by definition is college preparatory and not meant for everyone, will admit only students who can actually benefit from its program and do college-preparatory work."

"Revolutionary," exclaimed Mr. Glover.

"Astonishing," agreed Ms. Brown.

"And Mario made it possible," said Mr. Jones.

"Yes," said Bill. "And now the poor guy is in a heap of trouble. It's awful that someone who's done such good for us may go to jail." Everyone agreed with that. "If only we could do something to help him."

"One other thing," said Mr. Jones. "Did you see this memo that came out today?"

"No, I've been so busy." Mr. Carter took the sheet and read it, while Mr. Jones went on, "Have you considered the impact that Rod the God's ideas might have on us? All these new programs are going to cost money, and I doubt that there's much room for basing our admissions on brains in the diverse and multicultural world they're planning for us."

"Oh, my God," said Leo Carter. "I never even thought of this—I've been preoccupied with fighting the hockey empire. These people, these consultants, could ruin everything, couldn't they?"

"Yup," said Mr. Jones. "They've got the Headmaster under control."

"Then we've got to do something."

"Uh-huh. And as soon as you come up with an idea, let us know. We haven't got much time."

The meeting broke up soon afterwards, with everyone still quite depressed despite Leo Carter's good news. Mr. Jones went home and remembered he had a little piece of work to do before he went to bed. On his desk was a four-page form which had appeared in his mailbox that morning. He had only glanced at it. Its title, "Teacher's Report Form," was unenlightening, but perusal showed that it had been produced by the "Center for Children, Youth, and Families," and was being used by some state agency to assess disturbed teenagers. The name of the student whom Mr. Jones was to comment on was filled in, and the teacher was surprised because he was unaware that Julia Hamerow, a bright senior in his Twentieth Century Europe elective, was in any way disturbed, nor could he see why her wealthy parents had invoked state aid and thus provoked the issuing of the Teacher's Report Form to all of their daughter's teachers. But, of course, Mr. Jones would do what was required, so he sat down and took out his pen.

The first two pages of the form covered basics like how long one had known the student, what course you taught her in, her grades, etc.

Then Mr. Jones turned to page 3, and his jaw dropped. He beheld a huge list of statements, a list which continued through the bottom of page 4. There were 112 statements, and for each of these one was supposed to circle 0, for "not true (as far as you know)" or 1, for "somewhat or sometimes true" or 2, for "very often or often true." And the statements....good lord....

2.   Hums or makes other odd noises in class.
5.   Behaves like opposite sex.
10.   Can't sit still, restless, hyperactive
15.   Fidgets. (How, Mr. Jones wondered, is that different from number ten?)
28.   Eats or drinks things that are not food—<u>don't</u> include sweets (describe):_____.
29.   Fears certain animals ....
31.   Fears he/she might think or do something bad. (Don't we all?)
51.   Feels dizzy.
52.   Feels too guilty. (About what? And the "too" was sublime.)
58.   Picks nose, skin, or other parts of body (describe)
      _____
68.   Screams a lot.
69.   Secretive, keeps things to self. (I suppose I wouldn't know that, thought Mr. Jones.)
80.   Stares blankly.

83. Stores up things he/she doesn't need (describe)

_____

   The list went on and on and on and Mr. Jones was becoming confused about what it meant.
84. Strange behavior (describe) _____
85. Strange ideas (describe) _____
96. Seems preoccupied with sex.
109. Whining.
110. Unclean personal appearance. (Was "unclean" different from "dirty"? "Unclean" seemed to have ritualistic, Old Testament overtones.)

By the time he got to the end, Mr. Jones was staring blankly, and felt like screaming a lot, but he forced himself to finish his tour of this interesting questionnaire, circling "0" for all the items, and he finally came to the last item, Question 113:

"Please write in any problems the pupil has that were not listed above."

Mr. Jones printed, in large letters, "I can't <u>imagine</u> any problems which are not listed above," folded the form, and put it in his briefcase for deposit in the campus mail for the Director of Student Services to forward to whatever state agency had the happy task of tabulating these data, wondering, as he very often did, if it was he or the world which was mad. Poor Julia. She was a nice bright girl, earning a solid B, a good little historian. Mr. Jones wondered what invisible malady, what obscure curse, she suffered from. Perhaps the reason he did not know was that she was secretive, and kept things to herself? Mr. Jones thought that was an excellent way to be.

XXXVI. BRAVE NEW WORLD

The special meeting on Monday was one to remember. Dr. Glennis and his two eminent colleagues pulled out all the stops. Glennis also had along two underlings—apprentice consultants—who were kept very busy managing the charts, tables, overheads, handouts, videos, laser disks, and computer-linked CD-ROM screens of a <u>son-et-lumière</u> performance the like of which no teacher had ever seen.

As usual, all the material was presented so quickly, and was accompanied by such a millwheel clatter of tongues, that no one had time to comprehend it more than superficially. Mr. Jones was particularly interested in one big, multi-colored chart which bore the title Strategic Facilities Matrix. It had a horizontal row of boxes containing cryptic phrases: Goals (which were not listed)—Supporting Strategies—Master Planning Implications—Strategic Startup Consulting—Continuous Process Improvement—Resulting Fiblitte Weebdewo—Specific Eventuations. Below was the legend Strategic Alignment of Programs and Facilities under a big arrow pointing from left to right.

Mr. Jones shook his head to clear his drowsiness. The penultimate boxed words made no sense and he realized that he couldn't read them from where he was sitting. (He was sitting at the rear of the room, as the more cynical and burned-out faculty members usually did, because there they could more easily ignore what was going on, grade tests, make fun of the speakers, or doze, all of which were standard practice at faculty meetings.) But then, the fuzzy words made as much sense as the rest of the chart. And what was Dr. Glennis saying.....

"Our Strategic Facilities Matrix is based upon Continuous Process Improvement, as developed by Dr. Deming." His $275 laser pointer put its red dot on the chart. "You may have read his book." (Nobody had read his book.) "By systematic ongoing analysis of trends and benchmarks our Process Overview has prioritized the most desirable physical improvements, the most advanced pedagogical innovations, and the most significant and desirable overarching programmatic adjustments."

"Does that mean they'll finally fix the dorm bathrooms?" whispered Mr. Vetter to Mr. Spofford. His friend only shrugged.

"Our Process Overview mandates multifarious mutations in pedagogical policy and programs. If Mr. Cerf would please project chart B-7c ....."

Dr. Glennis explained that the Maypole Celebration had been expanded into a three-day Spring Solstice Jubilee, during which classes would be cancelled—virtually everything Broad Horizons recommended required cancelling classes—so the school could, in some unrevealed manner, "become attuned to the Infinite." The "eminently successful" hockey program would be greatly expanded by adding a "second sheet of ice," (i.e., another rink) and five more teams, one for girls. "We hope to proceed in an accelerated fashion," he said. (He meant "quickly.") "We will really put SLA on the map. And do not think for a moment that we are neglecting the academic program. Not at all. We will make your academics a beacon through P/R-type stuff. Also, we are urging the addition of Japanese and Swahili to the language offerings—with, we think, the dropping of German, a rather Euro-centric white man's language not in keeping with today's splendid emphasis on cultural diversity. There will also be extensive changes in the Social Studies curriculum, which my esteemed colleague will shortly outline."

He nodded towards the table behind which sat a formidable female figure whose raven hair, piercing black eyes, custom-tailored suit, well-filled Oxford cloth shirt, regimental tie, and hand-tooled wingtips had already distracted much faculty attention from the screens and charts.

Dr. Glennis ended his spiel and turned things over to Dr. Blither. He, a dapper man in his early thirties, had made quite a name for himself, and risen to his prestigious chairpersonship, by being even more radical and revolutionary than his contemporaries, who admired his dash and daring. Whereas most Ed.D.'s at least pretended to be concerned with what went on in classrooms, Dr. Blither did not.

"The objective of elementary and high school education," he told the SLA faculty, "is not the passing on of a few soon-forgotten scraps of grammatical, linguistic, scientific, or historical trivia. No! You will be amongst the first to benefit from proactive implementation of B-TEP, the Blither Total Education Program. Especially here at a boarding school, where you have such complete control of students' whole days, where you are presented with unparalleled opportunities for brainwash..., I mean for character development, you will be able, under my guidance, to mold your charges into very models of Twenty-First Century Persons, quick to detect prejudice of any kind, open to all liberal ideas, sensitive, altruistic, welcoming all differences, non-judgmental, caring, sharing, and, in short, completely liberated from the shackles of traditional 'education'."

He grinned fairly unpleasantly as he continued, "I realize, of course, that B-TEP may come as a considerable shock to the content chauvinists among you, those who are mired in obsolete and anachronistic notions that your main duty is to make students learn things, rather than to boost their self-esteem and appreciation of diversity, and who aren't aware that every student can have a successful school career and go to college. You may, for instance, find it a little hard to adjust to our abolition of 'grades,' but what are these grades and class rankings, if not a highly discriminatory, undemocratic, elitist, indeed racist import from the wicked societies of old Europe, which sent out their 'best and brightest' to conquer and tyrannize the nice peoples of the globe? There are no 'grades' in village schools in Chad, or among the native peoples of Tierra del Fuego! Yes, my friends, a fine new future awaits you when B-TEP is fully implemented at this school! The manuals are about to be printed from the discs on file at the Broad Horizons offices in Hartford, and you will receive them very soon."

If Dr. Blither expected applause when he finished, he was disappointed. His remarks had frightened the teachers badly. Mr. Jones was reeling and woozy, and the reference to "Twenty-First Century Persons" had his historian's mind running through certain twentieth-century figures who advocated the New Socialist Man and the Herrenvolk.

Now Dr. Mann-Hayter took the floor. She was about thirty-five, about six feet tall, about 160 muscular pounds, and, with her striking presence and unusual wardrobe, she really dominated the room. In a voice of complete confidence she explained the necessity of using every course, and especially those taught by the Social Studies Department, to "bring students to the realization of the historical degradation of women, native peoples, gays, lesbians, bisexuals, hermaphrodites, the transgendered, foot fetishists, the overweight, dwarfs, and, in fact, everyone on Earth except right-handed white male heterosexuals." She went on to stress the necessity of assuring that the number of women referred to in any class at least equalled the number of men, and that one girl in each class would be deputed to keep track of the teacher's references and report the results to the school administration. She explained the need to abolish "any courses which perpetuate the European imperialist-chauvinistic traditions, to the exclusion of true multi-cultural pluralism and gender-neutral, anti-oppressionary curricula. To this end, several of my most trusted colleagues from the Women's Revenge Program at Penthesilea University, where I hold the Catherine the Great Chair of Matriarchal Studies, will be here during the implementation of the FGP and B-TEP to conduct a thorough curriculum revision. It is essential to assure that we inculcate in the fledgling phallocrats here the liberating influence of feminist sensitization and diversity-oriented, omni-inclusional multicultural social studies."

"Furthermore," continued the eminent scholar, "the time has come to hire a female athletic co-director, one who can do for the girls of this school what Lance Vance has done for the boys.

My college roommate, Ms. Diana van Dyke, may be interested in this position, now that she has retired from playing football."

"I will be returning here early next year, with my colleagues, as the FGP and B-TEP get underway. I look forward to working very closely with you all, especially with several of the younger female faculty." She smiled broadly. "You will find in me no dreamy, impractical theorist. I believe firmly in a down-to-earth, hands-on approach in collaboration."

Dr. Mann-Hayter's presentation ended the meeting. Dr. Dukesbury warmly thanked Dr. Glennis and his associates for their fine work.

Mr. Jones by now felt ill. It was clear that, under the tutelage of these preposterous lunatics, SLA would be turned into a circus. But even as his spirits sank, he began to get an idea. It was such a wonderful idea that he smiled to himself and experienced a feeling of relief similar to that felt by the Duke of Wellington when he saw Blücher's columns approaching on the afternoon of Waterloo. When the meeting ended, he reassured several of his colleagues, telling them not to worry.

XXXVII. ENTENTE CORDIALE

Mr. Jones left Laud Hall and walked over to the Development Director's house. Clara, Mario's wife, let him in. "Oh, John, it's so nice of you to call," she said with a smile. "Mario will be glad to see you. He's been so depressed."

Mr. Jones talked to Mr. Pestalozzi in his study. He started with some routine condolences, then got down to business. He asked the man how serious his situation really was. Mario explained that he was not very worried about anything his consultants had done. "Nothing much will ever be linked to me, John. This FBI arrest was just a fishing expedition. Guys like Roberto and Alfredo never betray their associates, and I have a strong feeling that the really key figure, this Seamus O'Herlihy, is never going to turn up. Besides, the kind of legal help which the Family, I mean our consultants, is bringing in from Chicago is really good. What I'm worried about is that the Feds will start raking up my past and ruin my career here. I'll tell you straight, John, I've got some skeletons in my closet. But I really wanted to go straight when I came here, for the sake of Clara and the kids. I got carried away. But I swear on their heads," he said, raising his right hand, "that from now on everything is going to be on the up-and-up, just honest persuasion and good P/R."

"Well, Mario," said Mr. Jones, "everyone here thinks the world of you. Would it help if the entire faculty came forward as character witnesses? We teachers aren't rich or powerful, but we're sure respectable, you know: poor, but eminently respectable. I think we could sway any jury in your favor."

Mario's eyes brightened. "Gee, John, that would be absolutely great. It would be wonderful. If I can convince the cops that I've gone straight in the last two years, I'll be home free. But would your colleagues do that? Would they say nice things about an old Mafioso like me?"

John Jones smiled. "Mario, in return for a favor, a favor which will be of absolutely enormous benefit to this school, I will guarantee to get the entire faculty behind you one hundred per cent. All I ask in return is...." He leaned forward and whispered very quietly.

Mario grinned. "Oh, boy, that'll take some quick phone calls—but yeah, it can be arranged. My, uh, former associates are good at stuff like that. Takes me back to the days when I was a button man...I mean, when I started in business. Leave it to me."

"Great," said Mr. Jones. "And, of course, this will be our secret."

XXXVIII. THE CURE IS NOT WORSE THAN THE DISEASE

The pedagogical illuminati, having spent the night as guests at the Rectory, breakfasted with Dr. Dukesbury. The Headmaster was completely mesmerized by these people, as they well knew, even though, or perhaps because, he did not understand them. He was also very flattered to have so famous an authority as Dr. Glennis tell him that he, the Rev. Dr. Elwood J. Dukesbury III, was among the most progressive, far-sighted, and "futuristic" educators in America, and that the programs which Broad Horizons would inaugurate at SLA would make the school famous throughout the land and a prototype which others would envy and try to follow.

As Dr. Glennis took leave of the Headmaster on the steps of Laud Hall, the great consultant assured him that he would receive the first shipment of material on the Future Greatness Plan and B-TEP within the month. "Much of it is right here on disk," said Dr. Glennis, patting his briefcase, "and my staff in Hartford has the rest."

Dr. Mann-Hayter, pausing to light an enormous cigar, told the Headmaster how she was looking forward to reviewing the school's curriculum and making appropriate modifications. "We will really establish here a model for proactive, pro-feminist, behavior- and attitudinal-modificationary gender studies," she said. Twin columns of deeply-inhaled smoke gushed from her nostrils even as she dragged again on the foot-long Havana clenched firmly in her strong white teeth. She clapped the coughing man on the shoulder and went on, "Believe me, Elwood, when my girls and I get through with this place, testosterone levels will be pretty damn low—at least among the males." She chuckled around her Corona Maxima as she strolled down the steps to the waiting rented cars in which she and her associates would drive to the airport.

....

Alas, alas, the journey was not smooth. When he arrived at the airport, Dr. Glennis was paged and told to call his associate director at once, at his home number. He did so, and received the appalling news that the Broad Horizons building had been fire-bombed during the early morning hours and reduced to mere ashes. "It looks like Hiroshima after the bomb," said the shaken man. "The police say it was a really professional job. We won't recover a postage stamp."

Arriving in Hartford, Dr. Glennis discovered that all of his luggage had disappeared and that his car had been stolen from the airport garage. As he stood disconsolately beside the empty parking space, a taxi very opportunely pulled up next to him. He got in. A few miles out, the driver, who was never subsequently found or identified, pulled over, kicked him out at gunpoint, and drove away with his briefcase and wallet.

The cataclysmic demise of Broad Horizons was communicated to SLA the next day. Dr. Glennis said it might take him three years to rebuild his organization, if indeed he even bothered to try.

"It was probably those rats at the ChildFree Corporation. They'd stoop to anything to corner the market. I may just take a job with Dr. Blither's school and help to re-design B-TEP."

Dr. Dukesbury called a special faculty meeting where he announced that the FGP, B-TEP, et hoc genus omne, would have to be "indefinitely postponed."

That night Mr. Jones, who normally was rather reclusive, invited several colleagues to a little party. Mario Pestalozzi was the guest of honor.

XXXIX. GAUDEAMUS IGITUR

Every contract at SLA (except those of the hockey coaches) was for one year. Every year each teacher would meet with the Headmaster to discuss next year's arrangement. These meetings were usually held in late February. A teacher would get a note in his box asking him to meet with Dr. Dukesbury at, say, 9:50 next Tuesday. The time chosen would be during a free period selected randomly by the Headmaster's secretary, so a teacher might finish a class, negotiate his future, and hurry off to his next class immediately thereafter.

It was not quite true to say that faculty members "discussed" their contracts. One entered the Headmaster's office and sat in front of his desk. Dr. Dukesbury would spend a few minutes telling you what he thought your strengths and weaknesses were. He would then read from your contract, which had already been prepared, your duties for the next year; he would tell you where you would live and reveal your salary, which would usually be about three per cent higher.

You could then, if you liked, talk to him about what he had read you. This was a somewhat pointless activity, however, because the final section of every contract contained the words, "the faculty member will also do such other things as the Headmaster may direct" as well as the clause stating that the contract could be cancelled on thirty days' notice by either party. Since the school had no salary scale and no one had any idea what other people made, there was also little point in talking about compensation.

A couple of days later the Headmaster's secretary would send you two copies of your new annual contract, one to sign and return and one to keep.

If, subsequently, the Administration decided to change your duties or your housing, you would simply be sent a new contract and told to destroy the old one.

No one had ever tested one of these "contracts" in court. It would have been interesting to see if such protean scraps of paper had any legal validity at all.

The biggest problem for those teachers who did not plan to spend the whole of their working lives at SLA was that, if they turned down a contract and indicated they planned to look for another job, they lost their house on June 15. Consequently, many people who did plan to leave signed their contracts and kept looking for work; if they found it, they broke their contracts and moved away. This sometimes happened in June or July. The school had never prosecuted anyone who did this, but such unethical conduct certainly made things hard for SLA. (Occasionally contracts were broken more abruptly, the most famous case having been that of an Admissions Director who had gotten very fed up. A bachelor who travelled light, he had simply loaded up a trailer between two and four A.M. and vanished with the dawn.)

When John Jones was called in for his contract talk this year, he made no difficulties at all. Indeed he hardly listened to anything which the Headmaster said. For while sitting on duty in ESSH the previous night he had, between threatening the lives of some very unruly freshmen and giving extra help to some of his sophomores, reviewed the previous months in his mind. He realized that St. Lawrence Academy was his destiny. Where else could he do so much good, receive so much entertainment, and get paid for it all? Surely, he thought, if Franz Kafka had taught at a boarding school, instead of working in a boring old insurance office, what great masterpieces, far beyond anything he actually wrote, might he not have produced? And the time ahead looked bright: the Future Greatness Plan and its associated insanities were defunct, the school's finances were in excellent shape, the food had improved greatly, and, as for the remaining problem.....

Earlier that day Mr. Jones had been sitting on a bench in the Senior Corridor outside the Admissions Office, and, through a door left ajar, he had heard Leo, George, Linda, and Lance discussing an applicant.

"Gurk Maimer," said Linda. "Straight D's, IQ of 89, megalomaniacal manic-depressive sociopath, repeat sophomore. Needs fifty per cent financial aid."

"Just a real good hockey player," said Lance.

"SSAT score?" asked George.

"Last quintile."

"Reject," said Leo.

"But Leo," exclaimed Coach Vance, "if the hockey team has to have brains, we'll never have more than a second rate team!"

"What a dreadful possibility," said Leo. "Sorry, Lance, you know the new rules. Next candidate."

Mr. Jones happily signed his contract later that same day.

THE END

ABOUT THE AUTHOR

Brian A. Libby was born in Maine in 1949. He was educated at Cheverus High School in Portland (a Jesuit day school), Johns Hopkins University, the University of Massachusetts at Amherst, and Purdue University. He received his doctorate in History in 1977, his main fields being European military and diplomatic history.

After a year of complete unemployment he began teaching European history at Shattuck-St. Mary's School in Faribault, Minnesota. He arrived just in time to take a minor part in the revolution which overthrew the Headmaster. In subsequent years he was named department chair, was twice nominated by his colleagues for the ISACS distinguished teacher award, received the Board of Trustees Meritorious Service Award, and was named the first holder of the newly-endowed Cochran-Lang Chair in History. His proudest moment, however, came in 1984, when his students secretly collected contributions and presented him with a Franklin Mint replica of the sword which Napoleon had with him at Waterloo (in his carriage, intending to wear it upon his triumphal entry into Brussels, but something went wrong.)

By 1998 Dr. Libby's career had reached such a height of success and accomplishment that he suspected he was approaching a nervous breakdown, so he went part-time, and began to write. If enough people buy his books (or should he win the state lottery), he will be able to realize his current dream of leaving the educational profession completely.

Dr. Libby's avocations include computer gaming and classical music. His favorite composer is Handel. Both he and Handel are unmarried.

....

TRUTH IS STRANGER THAN FICTION DEPARTMENT

This novel is, of course, a work of mere fantasy. The author would like to say, however, that the documents, signs, and wonders quoted on pages 28-29, 64-65, 66-67, 88, 89, 98-99, 102, 104-107, and 159-160 are not figments of his imagination, but are real.

Juvenal said, "It is hard not to write satire." This particularly applies to education today.

CPSIA information can be obtained at www.ICGtesting.com
Printed in the USA
266720BV00001B/7/A